PARADISE VALLEY

To Kerry, her fiancé Ferdy is just a struggling artist — until he dies. Then she discovers that his family is one of the most influential in Spain. Then surprisingly, she receives an invitation from his mother Dona Elvira to visit Valparaiso — the family home in the Sierra Nevada. Wanting to know more about his family, Kerry accepts. She visits Valparaiso and confronts Ferdy's elder brother Carlos and his fiancée, Leora. Eventually, she learns Ferdy's secret . . . and also finds love.

GEORGINA FERRAND

PARADISE
VALLEY

Complete and Unabridged

LINFORD
Leicester

First published in Great Britain in 1975
Robert Hale & Company
London

First Linford Edition
published 2009
by arrangement with
Robert Hale Limited
London

British Library CIP Data

Ferrand, Georgina
  Paradise valley.—Large print ed.—
  Linford romance library
  1. Love stories
  2. Large type books
  I. Title
  823.9'2 [F]

  ISBN 978–1–84782–526–1

Published by
F. A. Thorpe (Publishing)
Anstey, Leicestershire

Set by Words & Graphics Ltd.
Anstey, Leicestershire
Printed and bound in Great Britain by
T. J. International Ltd., Padstow, Cornwall

This book is printed on acid-free paper

1

The girl who was standing slightly apart from the crowd was wearing a bright red trouser suit. Even against the gay holiday clothes worn by her fellow travellers she managed to look startling, which wasn't altogether surprising as her profession was photographic modelling, at which she was acknowledged to be fairly successful.

The slight delay between clearing passport control and the arrival of luggage was always an awkward one, and never more so for Kerry Loveday who was eyeing the sunshine creeping into the air-conditioned terminal, and she longed to be away.

She was tall and boyishly slim, with honey-coloured hair which hung heavy and straight to her shoulders. Although she escaped being beautiful she was certainly a girl who constantly attracted attention wherever she went; it was a phenomenon Kerry accepted but could not really understand, and even after three years in her profession she was not yet accustomed to it.

Almost unconsciously she fingered the pearl and amethyst engagement ring Ferdy had given her almost a year ago. It was a modest ring; all that a struggling young artist could afford to buy, but Kerry had preferred it by far to an expensive bauble bought by anyone else. She supposed she would have to remove it some time. Now that Ferdy was dead she could no longer consider herself engaged. His death was what had brought her to Spain. To lay the ghost, she supposed . . .

★   ★   ★

It was Kerry's mother who dispelled her doubts about coming, six weeks after Ferdy's sudden death. Six weeks filled with sheer hard work to try and shut out the heartache, but hard work hadn't been a very successful antidote to her grief. Kerry was beginning to wonder if anything would kill the ache in her heart. And then the letter came.

Very clearly, Kerry recalled that spring day. She had driven down to Elsingham, the little village in the heart of Kent where she had lived most of her life. Kerry loved her home village and enjoyed the visits she made whenever work permitted.

Her mother had looked delighted to see her and Kerry immediately felt the tension drain out of her. She'd been right to come.

'What a lovely surprise!' Mrs. Dalton had exclaimed, standing aside to let her daughter in. 'Come in, darling.' There was undoubted relief in her voice, even if her eyes did watch Kerry anxiously. 'You've no idea how pleased I am to see you.'

'I'm pleased to be here,' Kerry admitted, and her mother glanced at her sideways as they went into the kitchen.

'You've been working hard.'

'Long-standing commitments. I couldn't back out of them even if I'd wanted to — which I didn't. Doing nothing wouldn't solve anything at all.'

Her mother switched on the electric kettle and smiled sadly. 'No, and working yourself to death won't help either.'

'Oh, I won't do that.' Kerry sank down into a kitchen chair and stretched her long legs in front of her. 'I've not taken on anything else since . . . since Ferdy died. I might take a holiday now.' She sighed. Her head drooped a little and her hair fell forward to hide her face. 'I feel as if I need one.'

Her mother stood with her back to the sink, eyeing Kerry steadily. As the kettle boiled she turned abruptly to make the tea.

'How's Jimmy?' Kerry asked, mentioning her stepfather. Her tone was overbright, which didn't fool her mother at all.

'He's fine.' Mrs. Dalton set out the

china on a wooden tray. She glanced quickly at Kerry and then away again. 'We're both worried about you, but I don't suppose I have to tell you *that*.'

Kerry leaned forward. 'Don't be,' she said with sudden ferocity. 'I'm all right, Mum. It's just the shock, that's all. I can't believe it's happened, that he's gone.' Her head came up proudly. 'But I have a flourishing career and a good strong will.'

Kerry sighed again as she got to her feet. 'I'll be all right,' she reiterated as she opened the door.

Mrs. Dalton lifted the tray and followed Kerry out of the kitchen. 'We know you will, but,' she added, giving a little laugh, 'we still worry. That, I'm afraid, is one of the less welcome aspects of parenthood. We try not to make it too obvious.'

'It's good having someone to worry over me. It's an anchor in a mad world.'

They settled down in the little drawing-room, facing each other across a low coffee table.

'Has your landlord let Ferdy's studio yet?' Mrs. Dalton asked.

Kerry flicked a lock of hair from her face and balanced her cup on one raised knee. 'To two art students from Australia — two girls. They're very nice.'

She traced her finger around the rim of the cup, 'You remember my mentioning that I'd written to Ferdy's mother about his watch and the other little bits and pieces he left . . . ?'

Mrs. Dalton became alert. 'That was just after . . . You don't mean to say you've had a reply at last?'

Kerry nodded but didn't look up. Her mother sank back into the chair. 'I thought there was something on your mind the moment I saw you at the door today.'

Mrs. Dalton's eyes gleamed. 'So Senora Ramiros has seen fit to answer your letter after all.'

Kerry gave a very unexpected giggle. 'Not just *Senora* Ramiros, Mum. Dona Elvira Ramiros d'Alba y Santana.'

'Good grief!'

'No wonder she wouldn't recognise her son's engagement to Miss Kerry Loveday. That would have been altogether too lowering.'

On hearing such uncharacteristic bitterness in her daughter's voice, Mrs. Dalton said gently, 'It didn't matter when Fernando was alive, so it can hardly matter now dear.'

'She asked me to visit her.'

Her mother looked incredulous. 'In Spain?'

'Of course. You don't imagine Dona Elvira, and all the rest of it, would sink so low as to visit *me?*'

'I don't suppose she would feel like it. But it is a splendid idea, Kerry.'

Kerry let out a scornful laugh. 'You don't think I'd go, do you?'

'Why not?'

'Because she wouldn't acknowledge our engagement. She didn't want to know me when Ferdy was alive. I don't want to know her now he's dead! It's as simple as that, Mum.'

7

Kerry's blue eyes blazed as her mother answered gently, 'Circumstances have changed, Kerry. She probably regrets not meeting you before. She may be after some mutual comfort. Who knows?'

'And his darned brother!' exclaimed Kerry, refusing to be diverted. 'Taking him back without so much as a word or . . . '

'There was hardly time, dear.'

' . . . or a message.'

'I've no doubt they've had time to recover from the shock they're regretting it all. They'd have been too upset to think of anyone. It seems to me she wants to make up for it now, and I think you should let her try.' Kerry's face was still set in a stubborn mask. 'If you don't go they might never be able to forgive themselves. Fernando can't come back to forgive them, so that leaves only you. You owe it to them . . . and yourself. Aren't you curious about his family, Kerry? I know I would be — very curious indeed.'

'Of course I am,' she protested, 'but

they're such a disagreeable lot.'

'You won't know that if you don't meet them,' her mother reasoned. 'You *should*, Kerry. You did say you wanted a holiday . . . You'll probably decide on Spain anyway. Do go, dear. I'm sure you'll be glad if you do.'

Kerry's face relaxed. 'You may be right. I might have judged them harshly, I suppose. After all, Ferdy hardly mentioned them. I'll think it over during the next few days.'

★   ★   ★

Of course curiosity was bound to get the better of Kerry's rather exaggerated hurt pride. The indifference of the Ramiros family to her engagement had never mattered to any great extent while Ferdy had been alive. Now it seemed sense to make her peace with them before she could start out anew, free of ties or obligations.

Kerry crushed out her cigarette as an assortment of suitcases began to roll along the conveyor belt. Waiting for her own to arrive, she was jostled frequently by those eagerly anticipating a pleasant holiday. Just at that moment Kerry wished she could join them.

She felt lost and alone as she glanced around the fast emptying hall. Suddenly her heart leaped beneath her ribs, and she made to go forward as a young man came hurrying towards her. He was tall, with an olive-coloured complexion deepened by constant exposure to the sun, and his dark hair curled crisply around his ears and into the nape of his neck.

He stopped a few yards away from Kerry and looked at her uncertainly. 'Miss Loveday? Kerry?'

'Yes,' she said breathlessly, never taking her eyes from his face. 'And, of course, you're Ferdy's brother.'

'How could you know?' he asked in surprise.

Her face relaxed into a smile. 'You look rather like him.'

He smiled too. He looked very

young; far younger than she had expected him to be, and not nearly so formidable.

'So it has been said.' He looked down. 'You have only this one case?'

'Yes. I'm used to travelling light.'

He picked it up. 'Come. The car is nearby. You don't have far to walk.'

Side by side they walked out of the terminal building and into the sunlight which almost blinded Kerry for the moment. In London she had left a typically wet and windy June day.

She glanced sideways at him. He *did* look like Ferdy. In his casual shirt and brushed denims he was hardly what she had expected. He was altogether more approachable than the Carlos she had been led to expect.

'Carlos,' she said thoughtfully as they walked to where a large black car was parked. It was a handsome vehicle, luxurious almost, except for its dusty appearance; 'I do wish you'd left some kind of a message for me when you came to London after . . . ' He paused and looked at her. 'If you'd only left a note,' she added lamely. 'It was all such a shock to come back and find that Ferdy had died and you had taken him back to Spain, without a word to me.'

His forehead puckered into a frown. 'You are mistaken, Kerry. I am not Carlos. My name is Luis and I am Ferdy's younger brother.'

Kerry stared at him for a moment or two. There was a new feeling growing inside her, one that told her this visit was going to be more complicated than she had imagined. This inoffensive young man was not Carlos, the man she had regarded as her enemy, who had separated her from Ferdy even after he was dead.

They were standing in the middle of a busy road and at the insistent blaring of horns Luis grabbed her arm and led her to the safety of the pavement.

'I'm sorry,' she managed to stammer at last. 'I didn't . . . it never occurred to me. Of course, I should have realised that you *couldn't* . . . '

He placed her suitcase in the boot of the car and slammed down the lid. He turned to smile at her. 'Please don't apologise. It is a natural mistake.'

As he opened the door she explained lamely, 'Ferdy never spoke about his family.'

'That is understandable too. When he was with you he must have had much more important matters to talk about.'

She laughed nervously as she got into the car.

'You must not think too harshly of Carlos,' said her companion as he drove quickly away from the airport.

'Oh, I didn't,' she assured him, not entirely truthfully. His callous disregard for her feelings would still rankle even when her heartache had faded.

'You were not there . . . ' he went on to explain.

She half turned towards him. 'I was in Japan for three weeks, Luis, at the International Trade Fair. It was the most important job I had ever had as a model, and there was nothing wrong with Ferdy when he came to the airport to see me off. I had one letter from him in Japan and he certainly wasn't ill when he wrote it, or if he was he didn't say so.'

She took a deep breath, realising she was becoming more indignant than necessary with this young man. But the injustice of it all had festered inside her for weeks, and this was her first chance to exorcise it.

'Please don't distress yourself,' he urged as they came to the wide road which would take them into Malaga.

'I feel I must explain,' she answered in a more subdued voice. 'I realise it looked very bad when I was away, when Ferdy was so ill. I wrote to him several times but I only had the one letter back. I didn't worry about it too much because I knew he was never much of a letter-writer, but your brother must have seen some of my cards and letters and knew where I was.'

'Didn't you find out until you came home?' he asked in a very gentle voice.

She shook her head. The sea bordered one side of the road, and on the other side, another sea, a green one, that of gently swaying sugar cane swept for miles.

'My mother called in because she was worried at not hearing from Ferdy for a couple of weeks and she wanted to tidy my flat for me before I returned. It was all over by then, of course. She was the one who had to break the news to me.'

Kerry shuddered at the memory. 'Your brother,' she couldn't help her voice sounding harsh, 'had taken him back home. Of course it was the right thing to do, but I have feelings too and to him it was as if I hadn't existed. Ferdy and I were going to be married in October.'

There was a short silence. The fields of sugar cane were no longer to be seen. The sea was now out of sight and they were coming into the suburbs of Malaga where the traffic was much thicker.

'It happened very quickly,' he explained

when the traffic began to move again. 'A chill to begin with, I believe, and Ferdy would not have gone to bed to nurse it, as you probably know.'

Kerry stared woodenly ahead. 'He was your brother and you must have known him well, but you've no idea how awful it is to lose someone before you actually know them. I feel as if I never knew Ferdy at all. It was only after he died that I realised I knew next to nothing about him. It was almost as if his life began the day he moved into the studio.'

He glanced at her. They had to stop again for traffic lights. 'You mustn't feel like that, Kerry. You mustn't start feeling regrets now.'

'Doesn't everyone have regrets when a loved one dies suddenly?'

He drew a sigh. 'What has happened is sad for us all, but you have your life ahead of you and you'll meet someone else in time.'

She smiled sadly. 'I'm not being morbid, Luis. It's not in my nature. I have no intention of spending my life wishing for what might have been.'

'Good,' he said, sighing with relief, as they set off again, 'I was a little afraid, before I met you, that I might have you weeping on my shoulder for hours on end.'

They were reaching the centre of the town; its pavements were a welter of seething humanity. The streets were lined with orange trees, palm trees abounded everywhere in every plaza, and away in the distance loomed the Gilbralfaro hill topped by its Moorish fortress which dominated the skyline and brooded over the sea.

Suddenly she was diverted. 'What a lovely town!'

He smiled with pleasure at her praise as they drove away from the Paseo del Parque with its profusion of tropical trees and flowers and shady walks.

'Have you never visited Spain before?'

'Yes, but never this far south. I can see now I should have come before.'

'It is very beautiful,' he agreed. 'I did

hope you would like it.'

They were leaving Malaga now, climbing a hill road. 'Do you live far out of the town?' she asked as the road gradually became steeper, twisting sharply at every turn.

'It is quite some way, in a little valley in the sierras between here and Granada. Sit back and relax, Kerry. You are about to see some wonderful views of Malaga and the coast. This is the main road to Granada, Seville and Madrid. When the new road is opened journeys will be much quicker, but not so picturesque, but that is progress.'

The road was narrow and tortuous. The land dropped sharply away at one side of the road and olive trees, cork oak and eucalyptus ran crazily down the hill, whilst at the other side was a sheer wall of rock where prickly pears with their bright yellow flowers boastfully displayed, pushed their way through every spare inch of dry soil.

Kerry looked down to where the sea and the buildings of Malaga were receding. 'I remember something now,' she said as she settled down in her seat. The town below disappeared as they turned a corner and then appeared again when they emerged around the other side of the hill. 'Once when I first knew Ferdy I asked him something about his home and he said, in a funny kind of way, ' I come from a place called Paradise Valley'.'

'Yes,' answered Luis heavily, 'it is true. Our village is called Valparaiso — Paradise Valley.'

2

They had come to a small village. Every building was so white that it dazzled the eye. Kerry fumbled in her handbag for her sunglasses and popped them on.

'Have we arrived?' she asked as he came round to open the door for her.

She stepped out of the car and stretched her spine lazily. It had been a long journey up the mountain road.

'We are not at Valparaiso, but I thought it time for a rest. You must be hungry.'

'No, I had a meal on the plane. But I wouldn't mind a drink.'

A few dark-skinned children gathered round them but apart from those, the village seemed deserted.

'Siesta time,' Luis explained as they went into the cool, dark interior of the bar.

Kerry immediately went into the

ladies' room and she felt immediately better for the quick wash. The journey around those tortuous bends and the dust that rose beneath the wheels made her feel dirtier than travelling normally did.

When she came back a few minutes later, Luis was sitting at a corner table staring morosely into a half carafe of wine. She stopped in the doorway, once more amazed at his likeness to Ferdy, except that Luis exhibited a boisterousness of spirit his brother never had.

As she walked over to the table he looked up and smiled, and to Kerry it was as if it was an effort for him to do so. Memories too, perhaps.

When she sat down he poured some wine for her and she said, 'Luis, why did Ferdy leave home?'

Luis shrugged slightly. 'It was never mentioned. I was away at school at the time he left and although we exchanged an occasional letter his reason for leaving was never mentioned. I think it was because he wanted to paint and

Carlos wanted him to take up accountancy or business management, or something like that. Ferdy was always very sensitive; he could never endure friction, and so he left Valparaiso.'

Kerry tossed back a lock of hair indignantly. 'What is it to do with Carlos? Surely Ferdy could do as he wished. He was a very good painter, you know.'

Luis smiled ruefully as he refilled her glass and his own. 'You must find it difficult to understand. To understand you must appreciate our lives are run quite differently to yours. Our country for one thing has not been involved in international affairs for a very long time.'

'What has this to do with Ferdy and his decision to leave home?'

'Quite a lot, Kerry,' he said, and he no longer seemed so young or so light-hearted. 'It means we have not reached the same degree of sophistication as in other western countries. Children remain dependent on their families for much longer.

'We are an old family. My forefather came to Andalusia with King Ferdinand and Queen Isabella, and helped to recapture Granada from the Moors. As a reward the king gave him much land in the area and he built a house, took the most beautiful gypsy in Granada as his wife, and we have been here ever since. Life has changed only in the most obvious ways. Tradition is very important to us. And Ferdy, by leaving home and becoming engaged to you, broke with tradition.'

Kerry sipped at her wine thoughtfully. She was impressed but unmoved. 'Personally I think you have too much pride in the past. It is never as important as the present. But I can at least understand why it was not thought proper for Ferdy to be a painter — and why his engagement to me was received with such indifference.'

He cradled the now empty glass in both hands. 'Perhaps I can explain about that too . . . '

Kerry got to her feet. 'There is no need any more, Luis. It's best forgotten.'

She walked out into the sunshine again and stood for a moment enjoying the warmth of it on her skin until Luis came out and joined her.

In a doorway opposite an old woman, clad in black, nursed a tiny baby and eyed Kerry with a blank stare. How odd I must seem, she thought, dressed in my red trouser suit, here in a village that had changed little in a couple of centuries. Luis was right, one mustn't attribute twentieth century behaviour to these people. Their roots were still too firmly entrenched in the past.

Kerry turned and smiled at Luis as he came out into the sunshine. 'You live in a fascinating country, Luis.'

His eyes narrowed against the sun. 'In so many ways we live in the past. It is not always good. We are in many ways an unforgiving race.'

She considered him for a moment or two before saying, 'You are of a different calibre, Luis.'

He shrugged slightly. 'It is because I am the youngest, perhaps. I am almost of a different generation to my brother.'

A few moments later they were on the road again, travelling between ochre hills, beneath a blue sky.

'We leave the main road here,' said Luis when the village was behind them. 'The road is not very good I'm afraid.'

Here the land was flatter and groves of olive trees crowded in on each side of the road. Ahead of them rose the snow-capped peaks of the Sierra Nevada.

There was a silence for a moment or two as a herd of goats were shepherded by the car, hardly troubled by the mechanical intrusion into their domain. Then, glancing at her, he said, 'There were reasons why your engagement was not approved, and they were very valid to us, Kerry.'

She looked at him and smiled. The road was no more than a dusty track and Kerry attributed a fairly comfort-able ride to the admirable springing of the car. Here and there cork oaks were being stripped of their bark, a process which would not be repeated for another ten years.

'It doesn't matter now, Luis.'

'It does to me. I don't want you to think badly of us. I was very fond of Ferdy and I know you made him happy.'

'I wonder,' she answered with a sigh.

'Oh, yes, you did,' he said quickly. 'He wrote to me, too, to tell me about you.'

'He was very unhappy when he first came to London,' she said quietly. 'That was the thing that made me notice him at first. He seemed so lonely, even when he laughed and appeared happy. I don't think he ever lost that air of loneliness even after we were engaged, and he never really took me into his confidence. I suppose that's why I've come — to find out about Ferdy. Silly, isn't it?'

He didn't answer and a moment later she asked in a brighter tone of voice,

'Have you any other brothers, Luis?'

'No, Carlos is the eldest. Then there is Maria Consuela who is married and lives in Madrid, then Maria Theresa who is also married but she lives in Cordoba.' He took a deep breath and smiled at her. 'Ferdy was next and then another brother who died when he was two days old. And then I came last.'

'Quite remarkable. It must be very nice to have a large family.'

He laughed. 'But it is quite a small family by Spanish standards.'

'Yes, I do realise that, but it still seems large to me.'

His smile suddenly faded. 'Kerry, I don't want you to think badly of Carlos because of what has happened.'

She looked at him sharply, turning from the window out of which she was gazing at the acres upon acres of olive trees and the distant hills. It was truly a paradise valley. No wonder Ferdy was sad to leave, because she didn't doubt now that he *was* sad to leave his home and family. The closeness of the family unit in Spain was legendary, their pride was inbred, and Ferdy could not help but be part of that. It surprised her to realise he must have thought more of his painting than of his home and family.

'When my father died,' he went on, his face puckered into a frown of concentration as he stared ahead, 'Carlos became head of the family. It was a great responsibility, not just because my sisters were still unmarried but because he had the well-being of the village to attend to and our business affairs to look after.'

'Surely not?' questioned Kerry.

'Oh yes, this is how it has always been. My sisters had been betrothed for many years and so had Carlos and Ferdy.' Kerry's eyes opened wide. 'This is how it is still done,' Luis explained. 'Ferdy's future bride was Don Alfonso's daughter, Sofia, and she has a very big dowry.'

Kerry let out a long low whistle. 'Now I'm beginning to understand much better. In any country it is the same, Luis.'

'No, you do not understand. You are thinking the reasons are mercenary, but it is not so.'

'It's certainly medieval.'

'Yes, it is that,' he agreed. 'Life in our little valley has changed very little since Don Lorenzo brought his gypsy bride here in the fifteenth century. The people who live here still consider that they belong to us.'

'What happened to Sofia and her dowry?'

Luis grinned. 'The engagement of course was broken off when Ferdy left home. It could have been a terrible disgrace but it was agreed for me to marry Sofia when I am twenty-five instead.'

Kerry could not hide her amusement. 'You don't give up easily, do you?'

'She is very beautiful.'

'But what about love, Luis? That's the most important reason of all.

Without it marriage is just a mockery.'

'I do love her.' He glanced at Kerry. 'Truly, I do.'

'Ferdy never told me exactly what the letter from his mother said; he just told me our engagement would never be accepted and we would have to manage without their good will. I had the feeling he had expected no more, but it still upset him.'

'It is difficult to understand but that was how Carlos and Mama felt; for myself I was glad for you both.

'You must realise that, in particular, English girls are looked on with some disdain; they do not behave themselves very well in Spain.'

He gave an embarrassed little laugh and she said, 'Does that mean we are all the same?'

'Apparently to my family, yes. Spanish girls would never go on holiday alone, you see. They are always chaperoned until they marry. You are a photographic model and you lived with Ferdy . . . '

Kerry sat bolt upright in her seat. Two peasants, with brown wrinkled skins and accompanied by a brood of children, paused in their work to watch the car speed by.

'We were not living together, Luis! We lived in the same house which, I assure you, is not the same thing at all. I had a flat on the first floor and Ferdy's studio was on the third.'

Luis laughed in that embarrassed way again. 'To my family it is just the same. You do not live with your parents.'

'I did,' answered Kerry, calmer now, 'until I began my career and needed a place in London. Anyway, my mother was going to get married again and I thought it would be nice if they started their marriage without me in the way all the time.'

He smiled at her. 'My brother would not know that. I know you are a nice girl. I know that without being told.'

'Thanks,' she muttered disconsolately. She stared fiercely ahead. 'You know, Luis, I couldn't forgive Carlos for

31

taking Ferdy back without a word to me, but now I'm beginning to dislike him heartily for many more reasons.'

The car slewed to a halt amidst a cloud of dust. Luis jerked the hand-brake into place and turned, wild-eyed, to her.

'No, you must not feel like that, Kerry, please! I have only told you this so you would understand a little. He is not a bad man.'

'I never said that he was. But I abhor men — or women for that matter — who are totally pig-headed. It seems to me that your brother leads the league. He must have a hide like an elephant!'

'It isn't true. What have I done to give you that impression?'

'It certainly wasn't true of Ferdy,' she went on indignantly. 'He was thoughtful and sensitive. I think you are too.'

'Carlos has had no chance to have a carefree youth. He has had so much responsibility. It came too soon.'

'Well, if he wants to be old misery, he

needn't try to make other people miserable too.'

Luis sighed and sank back in his seat. 'He has managed our affairs very well. As I have said we have always owned a lot of land and when the tourist boom came we were offered much money to sell it, but Carlos refused. Now some of those hotels and apartmentos you saw when we left the airport belong to us.'

'What is Carlos's wife like?' she asked suddenly.

Luis looked startled. 'Carlos is not married.'

'But you did say he was . . . betrothed.' To Kerry it was such an absurdly old-fashioned word, but Luis did not take it amiss.

His face cleared. 'Oh yes, it is true. Leora has been like another sister to us. Her parents were killed in an accident when she was no more than a baby. Her father was a close friend of my own father and so she came to live with us. It was understood that she and Carlos would be married eventually. He has looked after her financial interests since my father died, but he has not had time to marry yet.'

'I can believe it,' Kerry said, keeping her face as serious as she could.

'But they will be married soon, I think. They have both decided on a wedding day, perhaps because it is time we had something to rejoice about in the family. Ferdy's death has naturally depressed us all. Leora was, in fact, very close to Ferdy when they were children.'

Kerry turned away from him abruptly and now the car was no longer moving she could see there were a great many brown-skinned people, heads protected by straw hats, at work in the fields.

'When are these harvested?' she asked, suddenly anxious to change the subject.

'Through the winter,' he replied, his tone more normal now. He too was glad of a change of subject. 'If you were here in December you would see whole families gathering in the olives. Most of the workers are now beginning to tend the almond trees. The valley looks very beautiful in the early spring when the blossom is out.'

Again the deep pride, Kerry thought as he started up the car.

'In a very few minutes we will be there.'

Kerry had an odd sinking feeling in the pit of her stomach. Travel fatigue she told herself. Yet she had made much longer journeys without adverse affect.

'What do you do with your time, Luis?' she asked a few moments later.

'I receive a handsome allowance, and do what I can to help run the family affairs and business. It is not very demanding.'

Kerry laughed. 'Unlike Ferdy, you show no inclination to rebel.'

'I don't have his talent.' He glanced at her anxiously. 'He was talented, wasn't he?'

'Yes,' she answered, 'I think so. He sold quite a number of canvasses for very good profit. A few paintings were commissioned which proves he was getting a very good reputation.'

Luis returned his eyes to the road.

'I only wish to marry Sofia next year and live comfortably for the rest of my life.'

Kerry gave a deep sigh. 'That's a marvellous philosophy, Luis. That's all any sane person could wish for. At least you have no desire to manipulate people's lives.'

3

The village lay straight ahead, shimmering stark white against the ochre hills beneath the glare of the afternoon sun.

It must be easy, Kerry thought, to remain in the past in such a place. The surrounding sierras virtually cut off the village from civilisation. Unbelievable to think that the modernity of a tourist paradise, the soaring tower blocks, the gigantic jet aeroplanes, were not much more than an hour away.

As they passed through the one main street of the village, into the square with its water fountain and small church, Kerry automatically put her hand to her hair. Peering down the little side streets she saw that they were no more than alleyways between houses built so close as to almost touch.

It took no more than a minute or two to clear the last straggling houses of the village of Valparaiso, and there ahead of them, set on a small rise of the land, stood the house in which Fernando Ramiros d'Alba y Santera had been born and raised; it was quite different from the modest studio flat Ferdy had rented in London.

The house had been built originally with a protective wall around it, and although the need for fortification was long past it still remained intact. The mirador, from which watch was kept in the days gone by, still topped the wall above a pair of enormous wrought iron gates, one of which bore the word *Casa* and the other *Ramiros*.

Kerry drew in a sharp breath as they approached the house along a dusty track from the village, and she smoothed her hair again automatically although it was not untidy.

'I'm surprised your mother asked me now,' she said and looked at Luis. The car had slewed to a halt in front of the gates and he stared back at her.

He said nothing and, as the gates

were opened by an old man who quickly closed them again once they had passed through, they drove into an enormous courtyard. Once it had been a place for keeping the domestic animals and horses, but now the ground had been tiled and no hens or pigs ran free in here any more. Half of the numerous stables had been converted into garages as a concession to twentieth-century living. It in no way detracted from the medieval atmosphere of the place. Horses were still kept, for from the remaining original stables Kerry could hear an occasional whinnying.

As they got out of the car the old man hurried forward, but Luis dismissed him with a few quick words and took her suitcase from the boot himself as Kerry looked around her.

As they walked towards the small gate which would bring them to the house itself Kerry glanced again at the stables.

'Do you ride very often?'

'It is easier to travel about the valley on horseback than in a car.'

'Nicer too.'

As he pushed open the narrow gate he paused and said, 'There is no need for you to look so worried, Kerry.'

She smiled suddenly. 'I hadn't realised it showed so much.'

'I am very glad you're here,' he said, with such simple sincerity that Kerry couldn't help but be moved. 'You meant a lot to Ferdy; you should mean a lot to us too.'

She pushed the gate open wider and walked into yet another courtyard. This was smaller than the one in which Luis had left the car. In the centre stood an ornate fountain whispering gently in the still afternoon air, and around it the most remarkable collection of plants and trees Kerry had ever seen. Overlooking the open patio on three sides stood the house itself, each upper window leading out onto a balcony.

Luis led her through the courtyard to the main door. Multi-hued roses abounded everywhere and bright red geraniums spilled from pots on every wrought iron balcony, garish against the stark white of the walls. The effect was dazzling on the eye, the perfume dazzling to the senses.

A small squat woman greeted them at the door. 'Catalina,' whispered Luis. 'She is in charge of the house.'

They passed into the comparative darkness of the hall and Kerry was suddenly chill. Her shoes clattered loudly on the cold marble floor and she felt, irrationally, as if she should walk on tip-toes.

'*Buenas tardes, senora,*' Kerry said politely in a voice barely above a whisper.

The woman did not smile but returned the greeting politely before she turned to Luis and they began a dialogue Kerry couldn't hope to follow. Kerry looked around her, at the sombre paintings on every wall, the heavy and ornate furniture, the richly polished balusters of the wooden staircase at the far end of the hall. She wandered across the hall to examine one of the paintings.

It was of a man in splendidly rich robes, the style of about five hundred years ago. He was very handsome, with full lips, and dark liquid eyes. With his small pointed beard he looked very much a Spaniard of the time of the country's golden age of conquest.

'Lorenzo Ramiros,' said Luis who had come up to her unheard.

She turned and smiled. 'I can see the resemblance — a little anyway. He looks as alive as if at any minute he might speak to us.' She laughed. 'I wonder what he would say.'

'This painting is by El Greco.'

'That accounts for it,' she said in some awe.

'The canvas is worth a great deal of money. We are fortunate we have never needed to part with it.'

Catalina was standing, waiting patiently, as Luis looked suddenly apologetic. 'I am afraid you will have to endure my company a little longer.'

'Well, that's no real hardship, Luis, but why?'

'My mother has been spending some time with my sister in Cordoba. Carlos and Leora have gone to bring her home today but they have not yet arrived.'

Kerry continued to look at him. She was tempted to think it a deliberate snub, but then realised she was probably being unjust.

The tension which had assailed her once more when she had arrived, drained out of her. She smiled at him reassuringly and he said, 'A room has been prepared for you and Catalina will show you the way. You can rest and freshen up before dinner.'

'That will be lovely.' She smiled at the woman who took her case and began to walk towards the stairs. Kerry followed her and then turned once more to Luis who was watching her. There was something odd about the look in his eyes but she wasn't quite sure what it was.

* ★ ★

Kerry sat back and was almost enveloped in the soft leather of the arm chair. The meal they had just shared had been superbly cooked. Kerry had no idea what she had eaten — some kind of seafood she thought — but it was delicious nevertheless.

Luis, who had changed out of his jeans into a more conventional suit, told her, 'Backward we may be in many things, Kerry, but our cook was trained in one of the best hotels in Marbella.'

On a glass-topped table in front of them stood a bowl of fresh fruit and a pot of rich, dark coffee. Kerry felt completely relaxed now. She had bathed, unpacked her suitcase and was wearing one of her best evening dresses. She had piled her hair on top of her head in apparent disarray, leaving her shoulders almost bare.

The room in which they were sitting was simply but luxuriously furnished. It bore the silent mark of money and good taste. Everywhere was the rich gleam of well-polished wood and the smell of leather. The floors were marble but the coldness was tempered here and there by thick white sheepskin rugs, and around the walls lights from medieval-style iron sconces shed a gentle glow to mitigate the harsh black and white decor of the room.

The windows and shutters had been thrown open to let in the cool evening breeze, and the curtains which, she had been told, were hand woven by gypsies, fluttered gently.

'There is still a strong strain of gypsy blood in all of us,' Luis said. He rolled his eyes expressively. 'It makes us very passionate of course.' Kerry laughed as she sipped at her coffee. 'But no doubt you've found that out already.'

She frowned as she returned her cup to its saucer. 'Ferdy wasn't at all like that. We had a very easy-going relation-ship.' His eyebrows went up a fraction. 'It was what I — we — wanted. I'd had too many intense involvements. They soon burned themselves out. It was different with Ferdy. I enjoyed just being with him.'

He shrugged slightly. 'You English are difficult to understand.'

'We don't conform to a pattern either.' She leaned forward. 'Shall I refill your cup, Luis?'

He shook his head and she refilled her own. 'Is your room satisfactory?' he asked as he watched her.

She thought of the comfortable yet functional room into which Catalina had shown her and nodded. 'It couldn't be nicer,' she murmured.

As she had hoped, there was a balcony overlooking the patio. The view when she went out there, of the lemon and eucalyptus trees, the hibiscus and rose bushes, the bougainvillaea climbing up the wall, and the gentle sound of the fountain playing, was incomparable.

As she finished her second cup of coffee she asked, carefully, 'What does your mother really think about me now, Luis? Has she spoken about me at all since she wrote?'

He stared at her dumbly for a moment or two and then, getting to his feet, said, 'I would rather talk to you outside if you don't mind. It is a pleasant evening and I think you would like to see the patio garden more closely.'

For a moment Kerry was too surprised at his discomposure to answer and then, getting up also, she made to follow him from the room. As they reached the doorway — the *sala* was some distance from the hall — voices could be heard in the hall some way beyond. Kerry was about to say something when she glanced at Luis. His face had paled considerably and his eyes were wide with alarm.

'They are back,' he said in a whisper.

'So it seems,' she answered, eyeing him curiously. 'We'd better let them know I've arrived if Catalina hasn't told them already.'

'No, wait a moment, Kerry. I must talk to you first.'

She continued to stare at him, laughing in a strained kind of way. 'Haven't we talked enough today? Luis, we can't stay in here *talking* while your mother is outside. It will look so odd. Your mother must be wondering where I am already.'

He kept hold of her arm but she pulled away and went into the hall anyway. There was just one person in the hall. He was standing next to the El Greco painting of his illustrious ancestor and although he was in modern dress and wore no beard the likeness was startling.

He was, at the moment Kerry came into the hall, glancing through the messages and mail that had been left for him in his absence. When he heard her footsteps, and those of Luis who had hastily followed her, he looked up. Then his face grew hard. Automatically Kerry stiffened too and her chin came up proudly as she was inspected by a pair of almost black eyes, as dark and unfathomable as those of Lorenzo. Oh yes, she knew just who he was without any doubt whatsoever.

There was sufficient family resemblance for her to recognise him as a Ramiros but neither Ferdy nor Luis ever looked so disdainful. He was wearing a grey silk suit and a cream silk shirt, hand tailored, and he looked remarkably cool despite what must have been a long, hot and dusty journey from Cordoba.

At last he drew his eyes away from her lithe form which was clad in her favourite emerald green silk shift, cut low in the back and the front. Never had Kerry been so aware of her figure.

Carlos Ramiros d'Alba y Santera looked at his younger brother and although he spoke quickly, from his tone Kerry knew that Luis was being questioned very closely about something. Luis stammered his replies like a guilty schoolboy, his pale face becoming redder as his brother's fury grew. Kerry had hardly expected a profuse welcome herself, but she was totally bewildered by this unexpected attack on Luis, although she could only guess it was an attack. The older brother spoke quickly but apart from the fury in his eyes and the sharpness in his tone it was not easy to tell he was angry.

Suddenly she recognised a very uncomplimentary word amongst the invective Carlos was hurling at his embarrassed brother, and in amazement she turned to him.

'He must be mad! He thinks I'm your . . . ' she swallowed hard, ' . . . girlfriend. I do believe he thinks you've brought me here for the night.' She glanced angrily at the older brother and then back to Luis. 'Does he speak any English?'

'Yes, I do,' came the immediate reply. His English was very good.

Kerry's face was hot but she refused to wipe away the beads of perspiration forming on her brow. Her eyes blazed as furiously as his had only moments before.

'You are abominably rude,' she shot

at him. 'Your mother must have told you who I am. This insult is deliberate and quite unforgivable!'

'Kerry . . . ' Luis said in an agonised tone.

'I am sorry, I do not know who you are,' his brother broke in coldly, 'nor do I wish to know. Neither do I know what tale my young brother here has told you.' He glanced at Luis scathingly. It was quite a devastating look too. He transferred his attention back to Kerry. 'I only know my mother and I were not expected to return until tomorrow. Our decision to come home today is decidedly inopportune for you both.'

Kerry whirled round on Luis. 'But you said . . . ' Luis hung his head like a penitent child and she turned again in exasperation to Carlos who was much more in command of himself than either of the other two at that moment.

'My name is Kerry Loveday. I was Fernando's fiancée.'

His face darkened again as he shot an accusing and an almost disbelieving look at Luis. 'So, you were acquainted with my late brother,' he said as if she had mentioned something of very little importance.

'I was his fiancée!'

'And the reason you have come?' he asked, not a mite more warmly.

It was Kerry's turn to look unbelieving, and then abruptly she delved into her bag, bringing out a solitary sheet of paper in her trembling hand.

'I have an invitation from your . . . Dona Elvira. Please read this letter. Obviously she has not told you about it, but even so you haven't acted with the slightest degree of chivalry.'

She thrust the paper at him and could have slapped the look of disbelief from his face as he took it slowly from her. How dare he doubt her! And how dare his mother not tell him something of so much importance. Surely she couldn't be afraid of him too!

'Kerry . . . ' Luis pleaded again, and she tossed her head back indignantly. She would have this arrogant fool grovelling to make his apology before many more minutes had passed.

'I'll handle this,' she insisted, staring fiercely at Carlos who was scrutinising the paper. 'I can speak up for myself. Your brother has an excellent command of the English language.'

'But Kerry, I must tell you . . . '

Just then his brother thrust the letter back at her.

'That is certainly nothing like my mother's handwriting,' he said to Kerry's utter amazement. 'It is a forgery. Someone has played a very unfunny joke at your expense, senorita.'

'What!' she cried. 'What kind of a trick is this?'

He gazed at her with disconcerting steadiness and Kerry was beginning to feel uneasy. 'That is what I am wondering myself.'

'It was *I* who wrote the letter,' wailed Luis. 'That is what I have been trying to explain.'

There was a stunned silence. Both Kerry and his brother stared at Luis.

He looked abashed and repentant. 'That was what I was trying to tell you just now.'

No one said anything and Luis looked up at last, imploring Kerry for forgiveness with his eyes. 'I found the letter from you where Mama had thrown it.' He looked at his brother. 'I had seen it arrive and guessed it must be from Ferdy's fiancée, or at least from someone who knew him in London. When I read it I thought it only right that Kerry should have her letter answered by one of us at least. The invitation to come here was just the result of what I wrote. It wasn't right for her to be ignored as if she didn't exist.'

Kerry just kept on staring at him; she dare not look at his brother. 'You fool,' she breathed at last. 'You silly, senti-mental fool.' Then, collecting herself she swallowed hard and forced herself to look at Carlos again.

'I must apologise for my presence here, senor. I took the letter as valid, coming from Dona Elvira.'

He nodded curtly. 'I understand that. The fault is not yours.'

He spoke as if he were a recorded message, treating her with less warmth than if she were a peasant. And she had been engaged to his brother!

'I am only sorry,' he continued in that same cold tone, 'that your visit must prove fruitless; my mother will never consent to see you.'

He took a deep breath and looked at Luis. 'You must, of course, accept our hospitality for tonight, and tomorrow I will arrange for someone to drive you back to Malaga.'

He began to move away as Kerry was about to voice some protestation. No glimmer of a smile crossed his face. 'And now you must excuse me. I have some matters that need my urgent attention. And you, Luis, I would like a few words with you now, in private.'

Luis made to pass her, shooting a glance of appeal at her as he did so. Kerry was unbelievably angry — not so much with Luis whose motives were good, but with his brother who could act so coldly in anger.

'Just one moment,' she said to his back as he walked away from her.

She started forward and he turned to eye her coldly yet again. She hesitated, discomposed by his expressionless contemplation.

'There is something else?' he asked.

'Yes, there certainly is,' she said, finding her voice again. He waited expectantly and some of her anger faltered. She was unable to hold his gaze. 'I don't say what Luis did was the right thing, but he surely has the right to invite a guest here without being scolded like a schoolboy for it.'

The worst thing was the way he looked at her before he answered. Kerry, too, was beginning to feel like a naughty child.

'I think, Miss Loveday,' he said in an almost mild tone of voice, 'we would not agree on what is right in a Spanish household. *Buenas noches.*'

He turned away again and Luis said softly as he was about to follow him, 'I am truly sorry, Kerry. I did not mean to cause such an unpleasant scene. I am a fool, perhaps, but I believed it would all come right once you were here.'

But Kerry didn't hear him. Carlos had gone but she still concentrated her gaze on the closed door.

'*Goodnight* to you, Senor Ramiros,' she said through her teeth.

4

Kerry awoke to the sound of someone entering her room. Until that moment she had been very soundly asleep. As she fought her way from the depths of her slumber she realised that someone had been knocking at the door for what was probably some time before coming into the room.

She struggled to sit up when she saw a young girl approaching her.

'*Buenas dias*, senorita,' she said gaily, to which Kerry mumbled a reply.

The maid set the tray down on the bedside table and went across the room, flinging open first the window and then the shutters. As the early morning sunshine was scattered across the floor Kerry mumbled, '*Gracias*,' and stifled a yawn.

The maid smiled even more broadly

Blue Anchor Library

Market Place, Southwark Park Road,
London, SE16 3UQ

Account: ****3183

- -

Adèle [text(large print)] : Jane Eyre's hidden story

Due date: 03/09/22

Paradise valley [text(large print)]

Due date: 03/09/22

- -

Total items borrowed: 2

- -

12/08/22 12:23 PM

and replied, 'Con mucho gusto, senorita,' and when she had left the room
Kerry gazed at the tray. A desire to eat
was the last thing she felt this morning;
anger and humiliation left no room for
hunger.

After her disastrous encounter with
Carlos, Kerry had had no option but to
come to her room. It was the only place
in which she could vent her anger in
private. There she had immediately,
and in great fury, thrown her clothes
with uncharacteristic carelessness into
her suitcase along with most of her
toilet articles. That little task took but
a few moments. She was still far too
angry to feel the slightest bit tired, so
she spent at least an hour furiously
pacing her room, smoking one
cigarette after the other, and silently
calling Carlos Ramiros all the uncomplimentary names she could think of.

Finally, when she did begin to feel
tired, and it had been a long day
despite her ennervating experience,
she undressed and got into the big

bed at last. But sleep did not come so easily. It was well into the early hours that she finally fell into a deep, yet troubled, sleep, which was long after the house had fallen silent.

Kerry flung back the covers in a defiant gesture and inspected the tray, deciding that she *did* feel hungry after all. The smell of coffee was very inviting and the rolls were warm and crisp to the touch. The Ramiros family may covet their isolation, she mused, they may prefer to live in the past, but they certainly enjoyed the luxuries of life too.

There was nothing primitive or old-fashioned about the way they lived in Valparaiso.

Within twenty minutes she had breakfasted, showered in the adjoining bathroom, and was dressed in a pair of linen slacks and a matching sleeveless top.

She wandered onto the balcony with the view of the patio garden she admired so much. Somewhere a maid could be heard, singing an unfamiliar tune in a high raucous voice. The air smelled sweet and fresh; the patio had been well-watered long before Kerry was awake.

Paradise Valley, indeed, she thought. It was well deserving of its name. And Carlos Ramiros, with his exaggerated sense of family pride, was the snake in this particular paradise.

She drew a deep sigh. Silly, quixotic Luis. How foolish he had been. As young and silly as he was, he must surely have known his own family, and be aware that in any circumstances she would not be welcome in their home. But she could not be angry with him. His motives were too good for her to feel resentment. Nor could she resent Dona Elvira's refusal to acknowledge her; Dona Elvira was an old woman. It was understandable that she should have inflexible ideas. But Carlos . . .

She stiffened as someone came out of the house, and then relaxed again when she saw that it was Luis himself. He was dressed formally again and looked businesslike, and as he came through the garden she called out to him softly.

He looked up immediately and his answering smile gave way to a woeful expression. 'Oh Kerry, I am so sorry. Please be angry with me and I will feel better.'

'I'm not angry with you, Luis,' she told him as she leaned over the balcony, 'and please don't apologise to me. Did you get an awful telling off from your brother last night?'

'It wasn't so bad. I deserved it and more. His argument made me see sense at last; he pointed out that Mama would be upset if she saw you, and I knew at last he was right. When I wrote that letter I was thinking with my heart, not my head.'

She posed against the rail of the balcony. 'Tell me something; do you think I would make an admirable Carmen, Luis?'

He laughed then. 'A very beautiful one, *carina*, but your hair is the wrong colour, I'm afraid.'

'I always wanted black hair. It's so much more dramatic.'

'It wouldn't suit you. You are stupendous as you are.' He stooped down and snapped a blood-red rose from one of the bushes and tossed it up to her. 'Try that one for size.'

She caught it in her hand and clamped it between her teeth. '*Bravo*,' he cheered. 'Perfect. I shall climb up to your balcony in one moment and make love to you.'

'Don't you dare!' she cried, as best she could while the rose was still firmly clenched between her teeth.

'Luis!' came a peremptory cry. 'What are you doing here? I thought you had already gone.'

The rose dropped to the floor of the balcony and Kerry automatically shrank back as Carlos came out of the house and walked up to his brother. So far he had not seen her.

Luis drew a sigh and answered, 'Yes, I am going now.'

Kerry had learned a considerable amount of Spanish from Ferdy and now her ear was becoming used to the sound of it, she could understand a little; certainly more than she could yesterday. Her lips formed into a scornful smile. She was certain Luis was being deliberately sent out of the way — out of her way.

Luis looked up at her again. 'I won't say *adios*, Kerry, just *hasta la vista*. We will meet again.'

He waved to her with a sad salute and hurried away before she could reply. His brother watched him go and then looked up at Kerry for the first time.

'*Buenas dias*, senorita,' he called to her.

'Good morning, Senor Ramiros,' she answered politely, trying not to think what a ridiculous sight she must have presented, clasping a rose between her teeth and posing against the balcony rail, as he came out of the house.

He looked no less disdainful than on

the last occasion she had seen him. He looked every inch the descendant of one of King Ferdinand's triumphant knights who rode to the final victory over the Moors in Granada, finally unifying Spain.

'I have sent for a car to take you back to Malaga. It should arrive soon. You will not have long to wait.'

He held her gaze firmly as she said, her voice heavy with sarcasm, '*Muchas gracias, senor. Le agradecemos su hospitalidad.*'

A flicker of a smile crossed his lips at the heavy irony in her voice, but he seemed untroubled by it, replying simply and with equal politeness, '*De nada*, senorita.'

Kerry's anger flared again at his ability to remain totally unruffled and unrepentant. Her appearance and presence in his house was awkward to say the least and his ability to accept it and dispatch her with such equanimity irritated her almost as much as his dislike of her had done.

She drew back into the room, crushing the rose beneath her heel as she did so. It was of some satisfaction to be able to leave him standing there. She went back into the bedroom and restlessly prowled around the room again, and after a moment or two she lit a cigarette and sank down onto the bed. In front of her, on her bedside table, was the envelope containing Ferdy's personal belongings; bringing them to his mother had been her purpose in coming to Spain. She had written to Dona Elvira offering to send them on, and it was to this letter that Luis had replied using his mother's name.

Impulsively she tipped out the contents of the envelope and watched them spill across the counterpane. There was a gold watch and bracelet, expensive, she realised at last, for the person she had believed Ferdy to have been. There was also a gold medallion featuring San Fernando, a ring, a silver cigarette lighter, and a pair of gold cufflinks which he rarely wore.

With an abrupt movement she tipped everything back into the envelope. She crushed out her cigarette and marched over to the door. There was no need for her to stay in here, hidden away on such a beautiful day, she decided. She had come in good faith; that there was no welcome was not her fault. The fault lay in the damnable pride and snobbery of the Ramiros family, who wouldn't accept Ferdy's right to choose his own wife.

As she wandered disconsolately down the corridor, her heels sounded loud against the tiled floor in the quiet house. It was a very quiet house. It was as if no one dare speak above a whisper. Kerry found it hard to imagine the Ramiros brothers and sisters as children, chasing along these corridors, squealing out loud in delight.

Now Luis had been sent away she had no friend in this place. As she went down the stairs and out into the patio garden she encountered no one, and realised that in her heart she was anxious for at least a glance of Dona Elvira. The formidable matriarch of the Ramiros family. The woman who had given life to those oddly assorted brothers.

The garden, as she had noticed the previous day, was in full bloom. The orange and lemon trees bore tiny fruit, growing in the constant sunlight, and she recalled that Ferdy once told her citrus fruit grew all the year round near his home. It was one of the rare occasions he had spoken of home, and the memory stayed in her mind.

The multi-hued roses were in full bloom too. In her mother's garden they were still in bud. There was a wrought iron seat in the shade of a mimosa tree, sadly without its beautiful yellow blossom at this time of the year, but green and shady just the same. Kerry sat down there for a while, with the fountain gushing gently nearby and the whole luxuriant garden before her, a mass of purple bougainvillaea contrasting starkly against the white of the wall.

She contemplated with no real enthusiasm her return to London; and work, she supposed. The prospect seemed less than inviting now that Ferdy was no longer there to fill the evenings and weekends with his undemanding company. His presence had tempered the loneliness she sometimes felt, living alone in a big city. Despite the success of her career and an army of friends, she had remained a home loving person. They were both lonely, she and Ferdy, she realised at last, both answering a need for companionship in the other.

It was some time later that Kerry wandered back into the house. She wondered where Leora was and Dona Elvira. Were they deliberately keeping out of the way? she mused. Had they already observed her from one of the balconies overlooking the garden and thus satisfied their curiosity?

When she walked into the *sala* where she had had coffee with Luis the evening before Kerry was almost glad to see a young girl who was wearing a pale blue nylon overall. She was polishing the furniture with such energy that made a rather listless Kerry envious.

The girl looked up and smiled as Kerry entered the room. '*Buenas dias, senorita.*' She indicated the leather sofa which smelled sweetly of new polish. '*Sientese, por favor.*'

'*Gracias,*' murmured Kerry as she sank down into the welcome coolness of the sofa.

The girl immediately gathered up her dusters and polish and left the room. Kerry hoped she hadn't interrupted her work. She didn't want to incur any wrath over *that*.

She had been in the *sala* only a moment or two and was about to have a cigarette when the sound of high heels on the marble floor arrested her. Someone was coming into the room. Kerry wondered if it were the maid returning to finish her work, but the girl who did enter hurriedly, halting abruptly when she saw Kerry sitting there was certainly no servant.

She said nothing for a moment or two — she seemed incapable — she just stared at the visitor. In looks she was a complete contrast to Kerry. Her skin was quite fair — pale almost — but her eyes were as dark as her fiancé's. Her hair was jet black, parted in the middle, and pulled back into a severe bun in the nape of her neck to show off the perfect oval of her face. Kerry judged that she was about the same age as herself, perhaps a year or two older, but no more than that.

The surprise on Leora's face gave way to an expression of coldness. 'So, you are still here,' she stated.

'Yes, I'm afraid I am,' answered Kerry, looking away. 'If it were possible for me to walk back to Malaga I wouldn't wait for transport, I assure you. It's no fun staying in a house where there is no welcome.'

'Oh, I'm sorry,' said Leora, looking shame-faced. 'I did not mean to sound so rude. It was just the surprise of finding you here.'

'The surprise is mutual,' Kerry said. 'I hope you don't mind my waiting in here. Unfortunately, I have no idea what time I am to leave.'

'It is quite all right. You may go wherever you wish. We even have a library. I cannot tell you when the car will arrive; it has had to be sent from Malaga as no one here is available to drive you. I would drive you myself only Dona Elvira might want to know where I have gone, so Carlos thought it best that I stay here.'

Kerry looked up at Leora who still seemed ill at ease. She moved about the room, clasping and unclasping her hands. She had startling looks rather than beauty, thought Kerry as she watched her carefully. Her figure was sensually full beneath the emerald green silk blouse and tailored tweed skirt that endeavoured to hide it, but failed. She would look altogether marvellous, thought Kerry, if she lost some of that tight self-control and wore her glorious black hair loose. In London she would be a sensation.

Leora turned abruptly and sat down in a chair facing Kerry. 'Luis was wrong to bring you here under false pretences.'

Kerry crushed out her half smoked cigarette. 'Yes, he was, but he didn't commit an unforgivable sin, you know.'

'Of course not,' she answered in some surprise, 'but our first consideration must be Dona Elvira. Your presence here can only distress her further. Carlos and I are most anxious to avoid that.'

'I do understand that much, but I don't think Dona Elvira is the only person in this house who doesn't want me here. In fact, it seems that Luis is the only one who does.'

Leora smiled weakly, her hands clasped composedly in her lap, but the agitation in her eyes, their inability to meet Kerry's at any time, gave the lie to her calm appearance.

'You must see you do not belong here. If you had married . . . Fernando; it would have been a great mistake.'

'We wouldn't have lived here. *That* makes all the difference to our chance of happiness.'

Her eyes flashed with fire. She was getting tired of being considered unsuitable for marriage to a Ramiros. In their own little valley they may be important, but to Kerry, in her world, they were not.

'You were to be married soon,' said Leora, her voice no more than a whisper.

'October,' answered Kerry, swallowing the lump in her throat.

'You were very much in love with him.'

Kerry refused to look at her. 'That is the usual reason for marrying someone.'

As soon as she had spoken Kerry realised that in Spain love was not always the first consideration. Possibly families such as this would laugh at the

74

importance she placed on love.

Impulsively Leora leaned forward a little. 'Tell me about his life in London.'

Kerry looked up at her again, recalling something Luis had said; Leora had been closest to Ferdy during their childhood. She realised then that she hadn't allowed for Leora's sadness.

'There is little to tell,' she said gently. 'He came to live in the house where I have my flat. We were always passing each other on the stairs or in the hall. That is how we met.'

Leora nodded slowly. She wore a large emerald on her engagement finger; it was a handsome stone but Kerry recalled that emeralds, for all their worth, were rarely unflawed. An appropriate token of a convenient marriage. But, then, as Kerry studied Leora she realised that no man would be sorry to marry her.

'I cannot imagine Fernando living that kind of life.'

'And I cannot imagine him living here.'

Leora stood up abruptly. 'Perhaps that is because you didn't know him as I did.'

Kerry looked up at her for a long moment before saying, 'I should think that is very true. I don't think I knew him at all well.'

The two girls stared at each other for a time that seemed endless and then as someone else came into the room Leora whirled round, and when she saw that it was Carlos who had entered Kerry shot to her feet too.

He looked as cool and unruffled as on the two other occasions Kerry had seen him. Some devil in her wanted to see him lose control but she guessed that it would not be often, and not very pleasant either.

He looked from one girl to the other, and then shot a question at his fiancée. Leora began almost to babble her reply, glancing hesitantly at Kerry and away again. It seemed, from as much as Kerry could understand, that Leora was apologising for being here with her too. What a tyrant that man must be! she seethed.

When Leora had finished her explanation Carlos looked at her. 'I am sorry your departure has been delayed, Miss Loveday. The car that is to take you to the airport has had a puncture, but it will be here soon. In the meantime you will naturally have our hospitality. Please ask for anything you need.'

She eyed him coldly. 'I'm as anxious to be gone, Senor Ramiros, as you are to have me go, so it will solve both our problems if you'll just lend me a car and let me drive myself back to the coast. I'll leave it at the airport for collection, and,' she added dryly, 'I promise not to run away with it.'

His face relaxed slightly. 'A suspicion that you might not did not cross my mind, but I regret I cannot allow it. The road to Malaga is an extremely dangerous one, even for those who are used to it.'

Kerry was secretly glad; she did not relish the thought of guiding a strange car around those hairpin bends.

'Then it seems I am your guest for the moment.'

'It will not be for much longer,' he replied, looking now at Leora's pale face.

She fluttered her hands in the air and laughed nervously. 'I must excuse myself now, Miss Loveday. There are many matters for me to attend to. We shall not meet again, so I wish you *buen viaje* and *adios.*'

When Leora had gone Carlos came further into the room, much to her discomfort. To her annoyance her hands were shaking as she lit a cigarette. It gave her something to do. She killed the flame of her lighter and forced herself then to look up at him.

'There is a flight to London this evening,' he told her. 'I have managed to obtain a seat for you.'

She returned the lighter to her bag and closed it slowly. 'That is most obliging of you, but I've decided not to go back just yet.' She was rewarded by the surprise he showed. 'I'm going to spend a week or two soaking up the sun — in Marbella possibly. I've never been there and this seems a good time to take a holiday.'

He looked at her suspiciously for a moment or two and then said stiffly, 'As you wish.' Kerry thought he would prefer to have her safely out of the country. A danger to the security and peace of mind of the clan Ramiros. She smiled grimly as he added, 'If you have difficulty in finding accommodation, please let me know. I may be able to help.'

'Thank you,' she answered, adding ungraciously, 'but your country has a tourist bureau which does that job admirably, so I'm told.'

He shrugged almost imperceptibly and then, after a moment's hesitation, eased the crease in his trouser leg and sat down on the arm of one of the leather chairs.

He looked at her curiously for a moment or two. 'Even though you believed that the letter was from my mother, I really don't know what you thought you could gain by coming here now.'

She gazed at him coldly through a column of smoke before saying in a very deliberate voice, 'I don't think you would understand the reason. It certainly wasn't for financial gain because I have a very successful career of my own and I live quite comfortably on what I earn. Incidentally, Ferdy's watch and a few other things of his are on the bedside table in the bedroom.'

He was still considering her carefully and the effect was disconcerting. Then he said thoughtfully as he stood up again, 'Until the car comes please enjoy the freedom of the house and garden. My mother will in all probability remain in her rooms today.'

She crushed out the cigarette in a huge glass ashtray which was on the table. 'And if she didn't remain in her room?'

He smiled slightly for the first time in

her presence. 'That is not an easy question for me to answer, senorita. I should hate to have to ask you to remain in your room. Fortunately, I do not have to make such a request of you.'

He was about to go and Kerry got to her feet. 'Shall I tell you something, senor?'

He looked at her in surprise and she went on quickly, too angry now to control her bitterness. 'I think you're jealous.' His eyes opened wider. 'Yes, you're jealous, because your brother loved me with neither your approval nor your consent, and you can't forgive that sort of independence, can you?'

His look of surprise gave way to a mask of coldness that previously might have daunted her. He was, just then, a formidable man.

'You are mistaken, Miss Loveday, if you believe I would want to manipulate his life in that way.'

'With Ferdy you wouldn't be able to

do that, but I'll bet you had a darn good try!'

'What good did his independence do him, Miss Loveday?' he asked in a soft voice. 'When he needed you, you were not there. I cannot forget that my brother was dying alone in that big city of yours. Where was the love you had for him then?'

Kerry gasped at such an unexpected attack. It was so unjust. She clasped one hand to her lips and involuntarily her eyes filled with tears.

'That's unfair, totally and cruelly unfair. He was perfectly well when I left London, but even so, even if I'd had to break my contract and fly back from Japan I would have done, if only *someone* had let me know he was so ill.'

His eyes blazed at her and she felt the tears begin to roll down her cheeks. She brushed them away with an impatient hand.

'But you wouldn't let me know, would you?' she threw at him. 'You were determined to ignore my exist-ence. Letting me know was too much beneath your dignity. You were deter-mined to take him back, even though he was dead you had to bring him here! Away from me!'

She was trembling convulsively now but she couldn't stop herself, nor could she halt the stream of hatred issuing from her lips. She had held it inside her for too long already.

'But just remember this; he was happy with me. I wasn't the one who drove him away from home and made him miserable. I made him happy again!'

She began to struggle with her engagement ring and almost dragged it from her finger. She tossed it across to him. 'Here you may as well have this too.' His hand reached out to catch the ring automatically. 'You already have everything else. There's nothing else left.'

The tears were streaming down her face and she could no longer see him.

Sobs racked her body. She made to rush past him although she had no idea where she could go, but he stood in the way and caught hold of her. For a moment she couldn't move, imprisoned in his grip, and then, shaking herself free, she ran out of the room and up the stairs, to the bedroom she had occupied the previous night.

5

The door slammed shut behind her and Kerry flung herself face down onto the bed. She buried her head on her arms and sobbed as never before. As the minutes ticked by the only sound to be heard in the room was that of her own crying.

What has got into me? she asked herself as the sobs began to abate a little and she felt herself growing calmer. Hysteria had never afflicted her before.

She struggled to sit up and pushed her hair away from her damp and sticky face. Spent and weary she stumbled off the bed and into the bathroom. The feel of cold water splashing against her face was good, and she kept on splashing it until her skin began to tingle.

At last she drew away from the washbowl and dried her face. When she lowered the towel slowly she saw that the face which stared back at her from the bathroom mirror was drawn and her eyes were filled with a bleak misery she couldn't bear to look at.

When she came back into the bedroom she felt completely exhausted, but, thankfully, she was now much calmer. She felt that it might have been beneficial to rid herself of such festering anger. Now the healing process could really begin.

It seemed odd to Kerry, as she wandered aimlessly along the edge of the balcony and back into the comparative darkness of the bedroom, to think that she and Ferdy's older brother should take each other in such extreme dislike. Between Luis and herself there had been an immediate *rapport*, and she and Ferdy had never exchanged an irritable, let alone cross, word.

He was so like Ferdy, yet so unalike. So much taller and broader, so much more attractive, she thought unwillingly. Ferdy had invariably dressed like a bohemian. He had been almost heedless of his own appearance, hating to wear anything other than jeans and a sweater unless it was absolutely necessary, whereas Carlos never seemed to have a dark hair out of place nor an unwanted wrinkle in his clothes. At the memory of those few seconds when he had held her in his arms, involuntarily she shuddered as if it had suddenly turned cold, and she could imagine even now the feel of his hands on her flesh.

The uncomfortable train of her thoughts was interrupted by a gentle tapping at the door. Kerry stiffened and froze on the spot, wondering if Carlos had come to enquire after her, and she resolved not to answer. The last thing she wanted just now was his polite concern.

However, the knocking came again, more insistently this time.

'Senorita. Senorita.'

Kerry recognised the voice of Catalina and relaxed again. 'Come in,' she called and picked up her handbag in readiness to leave. Her relief was very considerable.

'Senorita, Dona Elvira, she wishes to see you,' said the housekeeper in very careful English.

Kerry thought she had misheard, for Catalina's English accent was a very thick one. 'Dona Elvira?' she echoed. 'Are you sure she wants to see *me*?'

'*Si*.' The woman nodded her head vigorously. 'Come, please as quickly as you can.'

Kerry hesitated only a moment longer as Catalina went back into the corridor. She paused to gather up the envelope containing Ferdy's watch and other belongings, and then she followed the housekeeper out into the corridor, her mind seething with jumbled thoughts.

To her surprise Catalina did not go downstairs, but along the upstairs corridor. Kerry felt suddenly tense again. Dona Elvira was not supposed to know of her presence; why then would she ask to see her? And now the moment had come, Kerry was not at all sure she wanted another emotional scene, especially so close to the last one.

Dona Elvira's room was not far from the one Kerry had occupied. As Catalina held open the door Kerry went in very slowly, more nervous than ever now. Perhaps, she mused, Ferdy's mother will also blame me for his death.

The room was dark, the shutters still closed against the sun. When she first went into the room Kerry could only make out the dark shapes of the furniture. She squinted against the gloom for a moment or two and then started violently as the door closed behind her. When she looked around again Kerry was able to see that Dona Elvira was sitting in a high-backed chair at the far side of the room, which was furnished as a sitting-room. But she was still unable to see anything clearly.

'Please come in,' invited Dona Elvira. 'And please open the shutters so we may see each other better.'

Glad to oblige, Kerry hurried over to the window, opened it and threw back the shutters. As she did so she was very much aware that since she had entered the room Dona Elvira had had an unequal chance to study her. With the shutters open there was a superb view of the valley, the miles upon miles of olive trees and the imposing sierras beyond.

Kerry took a deep breath and turned back to face the woman who might have become her mother-in-law, and she received something of a shock. Dona Elvira looked formidable enough, sitting bolt upright in her ornate wooden chair, but she certainly was not as old as Kerry had imagined. In fact the only expected thing about Dona Elvira was the black dress she wore; mourning not only for her son but, as was the custom, for her husband who had died some years ago.

There was nothing old or pinched or wrinkled about her. Her hair was richly dark, although it was greying slightly and it was cut quite short, curling about her cheeks to soften the natural severity of her features. Her dark olive complexion was as smooth and as healthy as a girl's, and her eyes, as dark as those she had bestowed upon her three sons, were regarding Kerry with great interest.

'You wanted to see me?' Kerry said, somehow not daring to raise her voice above a whisper.

'Yes, I did. Please come over here and sit down.'

Her voice, compared to Kerry's seemed very loud. Her English was careful and very good. Kerry hastened to obey, and knew she was being watched critically all the time. The sensation of being under scrutiny was not a new one, of course, but being watched by this woman, being judged by her, did nothing to ease her nervousness.

'I have brought you Ferdy's personal belongings, Senora Ramiros.'

She smiled slightly. 'Please put them

on the table. I am known as Dona Elvira; it is one of the rewards of old age, and it will avoid any complication when my son marries later this summer.'

The older woman seemed to straighten up a little more. It occurred to Kerry then that this meeting might be as much of an ordeal for Dona Elvira as it was for herself.

She regarded Kerry from beneath her lashes and her hands, beautifully manicured and sparkling with several expensive-looking rings, gripped the carved arms of the chair. 'I must apologise for the trick Luis played on you, Miss Loveday. He is still very much the boy despite his years.'

'He has already apologised for himself,' Kerry answered quickly.

'He was wrong to write to you, signing my name, but perhaps Luis was wiser than I was when I refused to see you. Times have changed but I find it difficult to change with them. Now, I believe it's as well you have come. You have a right to be here with Fernando's family.'

'I wanted to come.'

'My son tells me you were truly fond of Fernando.'

'I think Luis knows how much Ferdy meant to me, Dona . . . '

'No, it was not Luis who told me, Miss Loveday. It was Carlos.' Kerry was more than a little startled and then Dona Elvira continued, 'I trust his judgement. I know my children,' she said, smiling slightly again. 'I know Luis is still very young. Luis's head is still full of romantic nonsense and a girl with your charms, Miss Loveday, could soon convince him of anything. It is quite different with Carlos.'

Kerry looked down at her clasped hands. 'Of course,' Dona Elvira went on a moment later, 'Ferdy told you his reasons for leaving Spain . . . for leaving his family home.'

Kerry looked up then. 'He never discussed it with me. I must admit I was curious to find out. Luis told me you were all against the idea of his painting.'

Dona Elvira let out a long breath. Her eyes flickered with some unrecognisable emotion. 'Yes, yes, that is true, but it was I who caused him to go. I alone, no one else.'

Kerry leaned forward slightly. It was the first sign of emotion she had seen in the woman and suddenly she seemed much more human, more approachable.

'Dona Elvira, please don't blame yourself. You above all others must know that Ferdy had a strong streak of wilfulness in his nature. The blame wasn't — cannot have been — entirely yours.'

Dona Elvira's momentary lapse — if, indeed, it could be called that — was over. She was in possession of herself again.

'Miss Loveday, if an old woman wishes to indulge herself in this way she must be allowed to do so. Tell me,' she said in a warmer, brisker fashion than she had used before, 'was Fernando successful in his chosen career? I never really believed it was more than a hobby.'

'It was very much more than a hobby, *dona*,' Kerry said soberly and then went on to tell her of Ferdy's modest success. ' . . . and Wardles have decided to show all his unsold paintings in their autumn exhibition.' She hesitated before adding gently, 'You have no need to be ashamed of what he achieved. For such a young man it was quite considerable.'

Dona Elvira listened in silence and when Kerry had finished speaking she said nothing for a moment or two and then her lips began to tremble slightly, 'You told Carlos that Fernando was unhappy . . . when he first arrived in London, when he first met you . . . '

'I was upset when I said that to Carlos . . . ' Dona Elvira looked at her and Kerry's quiet explanation died away. Then, without being able to meet her eyes, she nodded slowly. 'Yes, I believe he was, but I didn't notice it so much after a while. He never spoke about his home life which I did think was odd, but I assumed then he had no one. That was one of the reasons I was so glad to come here — to see where Ferdy had come from.'

Kerry was glad she had found the courage to speak the truth to this woman. Dona Elvira was not a woman to appreciate a comfortable lie, or for that matter, prevarication. Only the truth would suffice.

Dona Elvira raised her eyes to Kerry's face. 'And now you are here, what do you think of us?'

What a terrible question, thought Kerry. How could she answer it truthfully and not offend the woman?

'I really haven't had a chance to judge,' she answered at last.

'Then we must ensure that you do. You will stay and lunch with me.'

It was not a question. It was a command issued by a woman accustomed to being obeyed.

'There is a car coming to take me back to the coast. It should be here any time now, although if it were possible I would have loved to accept . . . '

Dona Elvira waved one hand in the air. 'The car has been cancelled. I cannot allow you to go just yet. You must tell me about my son. He was happy with you, was he not?'

'I believe so, Dona Elvira,' she answered, adding impatiently, 'but . . . '

'I will hear no 'buts', Miss Loveday. I know you are hurt because Carlos was rude to you. He often appears to be rude but it is not really so. You *must* stay here with us and see for yourself the place Fernando came from. I am not a wicked woman, Miss Loveday, just a foolish one who believed she knew what was best for her children.'

Kerry wasn't listening. The car was cancelled! All at once she felt indignation rage inside her. Firstly she had been summarily dismissed before she could lodge any protest, and now she was expected to stay without first being consulted on whether she still wanted to.

Dona Elvira may have suspected some of her feelings, for she said, 'Surely you came with the intention of staying, my dear.'

'For a while,' she murmured through stiff lips. 'Naturally I would have preferred to visit you earlier — with Ferdy.'

Dona Elvira let out a profound sigh. 'Ah, if only we were able to look into the future, my dear. How differently we should behave.'

Kerry was suddenly remorseful. Dona Elvira was trying hard to apologise; she seemed so anxious to make amends, so regretful of her harsh judgement of her son. It was only generous to let her.

'I have my own dining-room,' she said abruptly, getting to her feet. She was taller than Kerry imagined her to be. 'We will eat in there, just you and I together, and we will talk some more about Fernando.'

Although she was still a little

bemused Kerry had no option but to follow her.

'You know,' said Dona Elvira sadly as they crossed the room, 'Fernando should never have gone away. If he had stayed here he would be alive today.'

'You mustn't believe that,' murmured Kerry, hoping she wasn't to be, during her stay, the recipient of Dona Elvira's morbid self-reproach. Somehow that attitude did not suit the woman.

'It is true,' she insisted. 'Fernando suffered from a weak chest as a child. It was only our mild climate that prevented him from being very ill. By the time he was grown up we had almost forgotten about it and, no doubt, so had he. The damp English climate cannot have been good for him . . . '

★ ★ ★

Kerry was still rather bemused when she left Dona Elvira's suite later that afternoon. The woman was very reluctant to let her go, to such an extent that

99

Kerry was beginning to feel uncomfortable. From the extreme of being most unwelcome and a positive threat to Dona Elvira's peace of mind, it appeared that she was now very welcome indeed.

She went back to her bedroom when Dona Elvira retired for her siesta, and she was glad of the chance to be alone for a while and to enjoy a cigarette, to wonder what could have caused such an abrupt change of opinion. She was sure they had — or at least Carlos had — believed her to be a fortune hunter, intent upon forcing her way into the Ramiros family fortune using whatever method she could. Now she was invited to stay, recognised as Ferdy's fiancée — too late to Kerry's mind — but she guessed that was part of the Spanish way of things. Death to them did not sever all ties.

Kerry looked down at her naked finger. To her it could not be more final.

But she knew she definitely intended to accept Dona Elvira's invitation; she was still curious about Ferdy's background, still determined to discover why he had severed almost all his ties with home. And apart from her natural curiosity about these things, she liked Valparaiso. It was quite unlike any other place she had ever seen, and it was unlikely that she would ever visit a place so unspoilt by progress.

Belatedly she remembered, with some considerable embarrassment, the way she had flung her ring at Carlos. Now she would have to face him again after all, and it would not be easy, especially as it was possible her impassioned outburst had had the effect of changing the family opinion in her favour. That particular fact kept repeating itself in her brain, time and time again. It was Carlos who had spoken up for her and it was on his word alone that Dona Elvira had stifled her pride and agreed to see her.

Her suitcase stood where she had left it, on the bedroom floor, and in an effort to divert her thoughts, to clear her mind, she began methodically to unpack again. She hung each garment in the wardrobe once again, aware that if she were sensible she would have insisted on being taken back to the coast today, to a hotel where she could relax and soak up the sun, and lose the tensions that had built up inside her over the past few weeks. A place where her only consideration would be what to choose to eat for lunch and what dress to wear for dinner, where the men would be openly admiring or totally disinterested. No problems, no enigmas . . .

She was just hanging up the last dress, the emerald green one which had caused Carlos to look so disapproving — drat the man for coming into my mind again, she thought — when she heard the unmistakable sound of singing. She closed the wardrobe door and listened more intently. It was definitely someone singing, not a melodic song but a rather out of tune ballad; what is more, the man was accompanied by a guitar and he was not too far away.

Kerry hurried across to the balcony and peered down, for she was certain the singing came from the garden, and there, sure enough, to her astonishment, was Luis, playing a guitar and singing a sentimental song.

'Luis!' she gasped, 'What on earth are you doing? You look ridiculous! Please stop.'

He did stop then and looked up. 'Ah, I thought that would bring you out as nothing else would.'

Kerry began to laugh. 'Do you usually do this kind of thing when you want someone's attention?'

'As a matter of fact, I haven't played this thing for years. I had quite a job finding it, but I thought you would like being serenaded, although my voice is not so good.'

She laughed again. 'I do like it, but I feel such a fool. I'm not used to it, you see. No one does it in London — or in Elsingham for that matter.'

He propped the guitar against the wall. 'It is ridiculous talking like this, Kerry. Come down here. It will be better.'

'I'll come down right now.'

She turned to go but he said, stopping her, 'Don't go all the way downstairs, you silly, climb over the balcony. It's quicker. I'll catch you. It isn't a big drop. I've done it myself many times.'

Kerry peered over the balcony and realised he was right. 'All right,' she agreed. 'I will.' There was something of the child in Luis that she could not help but respond to. He was a very welcome contrast to his brother's continual coolness.

She eased herself down as gently as she could and although her appearance was one of lightness she was tall and obviously heavier than Luis had anticipated, and they both fell down in an inelegant heap on the stones. There was a moment of shocked silence and then, when they both realised neither was hurt, they began to laugh until their laughter turned into mild hysteria. After the tension of the past twenty-four hours, for Kerry it was a welcome relief.

Neither of them knew how long they sprawled there, a mass of arms and legs, laughing until the tears began to run down their cheeks. Each time their laughter began to abate they looked at each other and started to laugh all over again.

'*Dios mio!*' came a startled cry.

Kerry pulled away from Luis, whose shoulder she had been using to muffle her laughter. It took a moment for their laughter to abate and after she and Luis had wiped away her tears they looked up to find Leora staring down at them.

'Carlos!' she cried, '*Venga rapido!*'

There was no need for Leora to tell Carlos to hurry; he was already coming down the steps from which vantage point he had been watching the undignified display. From the look on his face it was obvious he found the situation as unfunny as Leora had done.

Both Luis and Kerry had sobered considerably while he crossed the garden. Luis quickly scrambled to his feet. He had discarded the tie and jacket Kerry had seen him wearing that morning. He handed a now very subdued Kerry to her feet and proceeded to brush the dust off his clothes. Kerry did likewise for the want of something else to do.

'I thought you were to be out for the day,' Carlos said sharply to his brother.

Luis shrugged his shoulders. 'I managed to be back early.' He looked at Leora and smiled broadly. 'Ah, Leora, you look delightful.'

Kerry hid a sudden smile as Leora drew in a quick angry breath. She did look lovely, cool and enviably unruffled in a pale yellow sleeveless dress, and not a black hair out of place.

She cast a meaningful look at her fiancé. It was almost as if she were saying, 'I told you so.' Her eyes, too, had a curious redness about them, as if she had been crying recently. Kerry wondered if that were so. If Leora had been crying at all it certainly can't have been over her, even though it was obvious she did not welcome their guest any more than Carlos did.

Carlos was still staring furiously at them both. 'Leora and I are dining with friends this evening,' he said abruptly, and it seemed as if he regretted having to leave without reading them both a lecture on proper behaviour. 'We must leave now if we are not to be late. Come, Leora, we will go and leave them to tidy themselves.'

Leora was slightly more glad of the chance to go. She exhibited no reluctance to leave and as she did so she shot a hate-filled look at Kerry. Both she and Luis watched them go and Kerry felt that dinner would be a more relaxed meal tonight because of their absence.

When they had gone she flashed Luis

a rueful smile. 'Have we blotted our copybooks again, Luis?'

He frowned and looked mystified. 'What is this book you are speaking of?'

She laughed. 'It's just a saying, Luis. It means we are in disgrace again.'

'For the moment. Dignity is everything.'

'Not to me,' she retorted. 'Having a bit of fun now and again is just as important. I can be dignified when I have to be, and I often am. It must be awful not to have a sense of humour.'

'Carlos has a sense of humour, Kerry,' he said, again quick to come to his brother's defence. 'It's just that he's very much on his dignity while you are here.'

Suddenly she asked, 'Why are you back so soon, Luis?'

'I wanted to see you. I *hoped* to see you before you left.'

'Actually, just before you started to sing under my balcony I'd been with your mother.'

His eyes grew wide. 'With Mama!

But why? How? I don't understand this.'

'Well, don't be too surprised,' she said, rubbing her arm. She realised only then that she had received a graze on it when she fell. 'Your brother spoke to her about me.'

'Carlos? After all he said to me last night! I can hardly believe it, Kerry.'

At his look of sheer astonishment she was forced to laugh again. 'Don't ask me why, Luis. Carlos and I had something of a disagreement, I'm afraid, and the next thing I knew Dona Elvira wanted to see me. The result is that I've been asked to stay for a short while.'

Her heart warmed at his pleasure. 'Well, that is *estupendo*! I will not question why because I am going to enjoy your company for as long as you are willing to stay. I hope it will be for a long time.'

'Now just one minute!' she protested. 'Remember you are engaged to Sofia. I think she will have something to say about that!'

'I cannot forget. In fact, I have been to see her this morning; I must admit it to you now. It was suggested rather strongly I should go.' Kerry frowned. 'To remind myself — as if it were necessary — of where my loyalty lies.'

Kerry still frowned. 'It sounds rather like a dose of particularly nasty medicine. Why should it be necessary?'

'Because of you,' he explained as if it were the most natural thing in the world.

But Kerry was becoming more and more perplexed. 'Me? I don't understand at all, Luis. What has your visit to Sofia to do with my arrival at Valparaiso?'

He took her arm and they began to walk in the shade.

'Ferdy was engaged to you and they are a little afraid I might feel the same way.'

Kerry still looked puzzled. 'But you are not Ferdy and I did nothing to encourage him to go against his family's wishes. He'd already left long before I even met him.'

'I know,' he answered soberly, 'but he was in love with you, and it's easy to see why.'

Her face cleared. 'Oh, I do see now,' she said bleakly. 'They think because I've lost Ferdy I might want to replace him — with you.'

He grinned at her and she could not feel angry with him. It was all taken so seriously. 'I realise you were being sent away this morning, Luis, but I had no idea it was for that reason. I assure you I'm not the least bit like a man hunter.'

He waved his hand in the air. 'It is of no importance.' He took her arm. 'Come along to the stables. I know you would like to see our horses . . . '

6

Kerry yawned and stretched lazily and fumbled for her watch on the bedside table. She sat up and peered at the hands. She'd slept well that night, far better than on the previous one, and it had followed a particularly pleasant evening. Carlos and Leora were not present, of course; Luis was his usual, charming self and Dona Elvira seemed to have lost her initial stiffness and was charming too. She had proved to be a very intelligent and entertaining hostess, although she never lost an iota of her dignity.

Kerry opened the shutters wide and the curtains fluttered in a gentle breeze. Now she was ready to enjoy another day and she had awoken early enough to wallow in a leisurely bath before the maid was due to bring breakfast.

She was just coming out of the

bathroom when the maid came in with the tray. The coffee smelled inviting and the rolls were crisp and crumbly again.

When she was dressed she ventured out on to the balcony again. This morning Kerry was anxious not to monopolise Luis more than was absolutely necessary. If Carlos feared, or suspected, that his brother may be infatuated with her and that she would encourage him, she didn't really care. In fact it would have given her a great deal of pleasure to annoy him in this way, but she appreciated that Luis himself did have a strong streak of the romantic in him and it was entirely possible that he would become — if only temporarily — infatuated with her. For her own sake as well as his she wanted to avoid that, and the unpleasant consequences which would result.

But it wasn't Luis she saw in the garden. Kerry had been standing on the balcony some few minutes, enjoying the air which was at its freshest at this time of the morning.

A movement down below caught her eye. It gave her something of a shock to see Leora, dressed in tight black trousers, matching bolero, white blouse, and the black wide-brimmed Cordoban sombrero which still remained as the official riding habit in Spain. She looked more than ever very Spanish and very lovely, and once again Kerry realised her coming marriage would not be one of convenience alone.

Leora's crooked arm was filled with roses — all of them red — a bloom that was very much her flower. Kerry watched her for a while, marvelling that she was every inch a proper wife for a man like Carlos; it was a role she had been groomed to fulfil since childhood.

She snipped another rose and then straightened up. When she raised her eyes slowly to look up, Kerry realised that Leora had known she was there, probably for quite some time.

'*Buenas dias*,' said Kerry brightly. 'Your roses are beautiful.'

'Thank you,' she answered formally.

'They are at their best at this time of the year.'

She turned away and Kerry said quickly. 'Are they for the house? Some people are very clever at arranging them.'

'No, they are for Fernando. I take them to him every day.'

She didn't look up as she spoke and her words, for a moment, gave Kerry a shock. When she tried to answer she found her throat had gone dry and her voice was no more than a harsh whisper.

'To the church?'

'I go every day,' she repeated, and then she looked at Kerry again, challenging her with her eyes.

Kerry hesitated to ask for a moment and then ventured, 'May I come with you today, Leora? I'd very much like to.'

Leora was noticeably reluctant. 'If you wish,' she said at last and then, eyeing Kerry's cotton dress, 'You should have some covering for your head. The sun is deceptively strong and even we, who live here, respect it.'

'I have a floppy straw hat. Will that do?'

Leora answered with only an inclination of her head, but then, looking at Kerry again, said, 'We shall ride there so if you wish to change, please do so now.'

'I'll only take a minute or two,' she assured Leora who eyed her coldly and said in all seriousness, 'It doesn't matter as long as you come down by way of the stairs.'

Kerry turned away quickly lest Leora should see the grin the reminder of that episode invoked. It was impossible even to try and imagine either Carlos or Leora doing something as impulsive or ridiculous.

She ran back into the room, threw off her dress and rummaged in the wardrobe for a pair of denims and a shirt. When she was dressed again Kerry glanced quickly in the mirror. As she crammed the hat on top of her carefully arranged hair she thought how ridiculous she looked, especially against Leora's immaculate appearance, but had no chance to improve on her own.

Kerry badly wanted to be friends with Leora. Leora had been close to Ferdy as they grew up together, and therefore it was certain that Ferdy had loved Leora in return. Kerry felt no jealousy even in the knowledge that Leora knew Ferdy far better than she had done, but she had the feeling that, unreasonably, Leora was a little jealous of her.

Leora was waiting, motionless like a statue, in the garden when Kerry came hurrying out of the house. If she disapproved of Kerry's unconventional garb, or even noticed it, she made no sign. The moment Kerry appeared she began to walk briskly towards the gate so that Kerry had to run to catch up with her.

As they crossed the large courtyard, going towards the stables, Leora walked stiffly, staring straight ahead of her. The armful of roses she carried looked an incongruous and vivid splash of colour against the deep black of her suit. It was almost like a pool of blood and Kerry felt momentarily cold.

'You are, I believe,' she ventured in as bright a tone as she could manage, 'to be married soon.'

'In September,' Leora answered with no perceptible thawing of her manner.

'You must be excited at the prospect,' insisted Kerry still using her brightest tone. She was determined not to be deterred by Leora's distant manner, certain that the girl, beneath a cold façade, could be warm and friendly too. 'There is always such a lot to do before a wedding; arrangements to be made, clothes to buy.'

'It has been planned for a long time,' she answered.

'Oh yes, Luis did explain that you've been engaged for a long time.'

She looked at Kerry then. 'It is not quite the same thing in Spain.'

'I realise that. I must admit it seems a

very odd arrangement to me.'

'Very often the choice is not ours but the result is more favourable eventually.' She stopped walking and looked at Kerry again, more searchingly this time. 'This way it is certain that a couple are well-matched in every way.'

Kerry held her gaze. 'Particularly financially.'

Leora smiled at last. 'Yes, but also we grow up knowing whom we are to marry, and we can both learn as we grow older what is necessary to make the marriage successful. It obviates a lot of problems.'

'And pleasures.'

Leora began to walk towards the stables again and Kerry had to hurry to catch up once more. Leora's horse, a handsome chestnut mare, was already saddled and they had to wait a minute or two for one to be saddled for Kerry. Leora climbed up on hers immediately and seemed to enjoy looking down on the other girl.

'You find our customs odd, don't

you?' she said, smiling scornfully.

'I must admit that I do. I can't believe that perfection is so easily accomplished. Nature being a very human thing is not perfect; there must be many people who rebel against arranged marriages and fall in love with someone else. As I said, it's only human nature.'

Leora's face hardened, her eyes flashed with fire, and she spurred her horse sharply, causing Kerry to step back abruptly as the animal charged past. Kerry recovered herself almost immediately and mounted the mare that had been made ready for her, and she galloped into the courtyard through the tall gateway after Leora.

★ ★ ★

The roses were already wilting. Kerry wondered why Leora hadn't realised they would. The roses she had left yesterday were dead and shrivelled and she removed them carefully. To Kerry the gesture of fresh flowers each day in this hot land was moving but futile. She doubted if she could be as devoted herself, and it justified her belief that Leora was not the unresponsive person she would have everyone believe.

Leora had slowed her horse halfway down the road to the village, allowing Kerry to catch up with her, but not another word had been exchanged between them. They had passed through the village, watched by silent and curious villagers, the men removing their hats as the two horsewomen passed, the women and children shrinking back out of the way.

'Do you think you should come here so often, Leora?' Kerry asked after a few minutes when she could endure the silence between them no longer.

Leora raised her eyes slowly. 'Do you resent my coming here?'

Kerry was too taken aback to answer for a moment or two, and then she stammered, 'Of course I don't. It never occurred to me to *resent* you. I just thought it would be best for you if you didn't come here quite so often. You are only upsetting yourself unnecessarily and you don't really need to come to remember Ferdy. I shall never forget him wherever I am, whatever I do in the future.'

To Kerry's further surprise Leora covered her face with her hands and began to cry, very softly, very gently. Kerry put her arm around Leora's shaking shoulders, trying hard to hide her own distress.

'Oh, please don't cry,' she begged. 'If I'd known this would happen I wouldn't have said anything. I'm sorry; really I am. You must miss him most of all. Childhood friends always do have a special place in one's affections, don't they?'

Leora pulled away at last. 'You know nothing about it,' she murmured and began to dry her eyes on a small scrap of handkerchief. Kerry watched her anxiously. Leora's tears were both surprising and welcome; it had proved she was human beneath that cold exterior. Kerry had suspected as much all the time.

Then Leora looked at her at last. There was no sign on her face of those heartbroken tears.

'Did he ever speak of me?'

Kerry hesitated to answer. She slipped on her sunglasses and turned away. 'He never discussed his home.' Leora made no reply and Kerry went on quickly, 'Shall we go back now, Leora?'

As they rode in silence through the village Kerry eyed her companion covertly. Leora was now totally composed and Kerry marvelled at how complex were this girl's emotions. She wondered, too, if Ferdy had been as fond of Leora as she was of him. It seemed logical to suppose he might have been reasonably fond of the girl who was almost a sister to him, but Leora's affection seemed more than just that; it had something of idolatry in it. And this was understandable too. Leora and Ferdy were the closest in age, yet Ferdy must have been two or three years older which might inspire an undying hero-worship.

The road to Casa Ramiros stretched dustily ahead of them. Against a backdrop of ochre hills rose the stark white walls of the outer-courtyard and its now blind mirador. The horse saddled for Kerry was a placid one and easy to ride. She was glad of the opportunity to ride. It was easier to see the surrounding countryside from the saddle, the strange, silvery boughs of the olive trees which meant so much prosperity for the region. And riding was one pursuit she had always enjoyed and never found enough time to pursue since her move to London. Sometimes she and Ferdy hired mounts and rode through Hyde Park, but it wasn't the same.

Leora glanced sideways at Kerry who averted her curious gaze. 'How long do you intend to stay?' she asked abruptly. It was the first time anyone had asked that question, which was odd now that Kerry came to consider it.

'No more than a fortnight,' she answered.

Leora looked dismayed. 'So long?'

Kerry could not help but laugh. 'It may not be. No one has mentioned a time limit but Dona Elvira wants me to stay for a while and it would be rude of me to rush away. Besides I have nothing to rush home to; no pressing engagements at the moment.'

'Now that you are accepted as Fernando's fiancée, Dona Elvira will not want you to go,' Leora said carefully.

Kerry looked at her in astonishment but the girl kept her eyes on the road ahead.

'I'm not sure I understand.'

Leora turned and smiled enigmatically. 'You have gained her approval.'

'Well, I'm glad of that, naturally, but . . . '

'Her daughters are married and living away. Soon Carlos and I will be married and then Luis and Sofia . . . She will be alone. You are all she has left of Fernando and she will be reluctant to let you go.'

Suddenly Kerry understood. 'For good? Oh no, that's impossible. I have a career and a home in London. I wouldn't want to stay here. Besides, I shall want to get married one day.'

Leora looked at Kerry and her face was filled with dismay. The horses were moving very slowly. The sun was climbing higher in the sky and burning through the thin material of her shirt. She was glad she had been told to wear a hat. The little valley was a natural suntrap.

'You didn't love Fernando,' she stated.

'Of course I did.' She hesitated. 'I doubt if I could make you understand, Leora; your attitude to such matters is quite different to mine. It's not impossible to love more than once in a lifetime. My own mother has been happily married twice.'

Leora looked away and nodded slowly. 'Yes, you are right. At least I hope you are right.'

She spurred her horse on faster and cantered ahead of Kerry who made no attempt to catch up with her. But Leora did not ride far. She came to a halt about two hundred yards from the house and when Kerry caught up with her she had dismounted and was talking in an uncharacteristically agitated way to an old woman, dressed in black, who had come out of the house.

Leora looked both angry and upset and was speaking so quickly Kerry couldn't understand a word of what she was saying. The woman had a deeply wrinkled face which made her look old but Kerry doubted if she were more than mid-fifty. Grasping the old woman's hand was a child, a boy of four or five, brown-skinned and sturdy. When Kerry rode up Leora stopped speaking and the woman replied in an equally rapid manner which was just as incomprehensible to Kerry. But several times she heard Dona Elvira's name mentioned.

'What was all that about?' asked Kerry when the woman and boy had set off on their walk back to the village, the child looking back regretfully at the two splendid horses.

Leora remounted and followed them with her eyes, and then twisted back into the saddle. 'I'm sorry,' she said blankly, turning to glance at them again. 'Did you say something?'

Leora was more than a little preoccupied. Kerry laughed, a little selfconsciously. 'I was just wondering if anything was wrong. You seem upset.'

Leora smiled brightly but it seemed false to Kerry who was watching her closely. 'Wrong? Of course not.' It seemed as she started to ride again that she was not going to say any more, but then she suddenly changed her mind. 'The older members of the village still run to Dona Elvira with their little problems. I am very anxious to protect her from that at the moment.'

It was logical, thought Kerry, but somehow she didn't believe her.

They rode into the courtyard, dismounted and handed their horses to the man in charge of the stables.

'Is the old woman Roberto's mother?' Kerry asked as they walked back across the courtyard.

'No,' answered Leora sharply. 'His parents are dead. Senora Penaro has no children of her own. It is a great tragedy so she looks after Roberto. She is devoted to him.'

As they passed through the second gateway the scent of roses met them, almost forcibly.

'I had the oddest feeling,' mused Kerry, 'when I looked at that child . . . ' Leora stopped in the centre of the garden. The fountain hissed gently behind her. Kerry's face cleared. 'He had a very strong look of the Ramiros family.'

Leora continued to stare at her until it became almost uncomfortable, and then she looked away. 'That is very possible. In the old days it was customary for the *don* to demand every kind of service from his servants, and they all were that in those days.' She looked at Kerry and smiled now. 'You will no doubt notice many of the older people too with such characteristics.'

'Is it still the custom?' Kerry felt bound to ask.

Leora looked so irritatingly condescending Kerry just wanted to ruffle her calm. But it was not to be. Leora just smiled again and said, 'If it is, I would not be told about it.' She frowned a little then and passed the back of her hand across her brow. 'I must go and change now. You will excuse me.'

Kerry stayed where she was, watching Leora as she went back into the house. What an enigma that girl was. She could only hope that Carlos, having known her from childhood, found her easier to understand.

She began to wander back towards the house herself but had only reached the third step when she paused thoughtfully. Carlos. Yes, that was who Roberto looked like. Carlos. It was more than just a likeness. It was the line of his mouth, the cast of his head, the way he had of looking at her, even the smile. She stood as if mesmerised. Was it possible? Did he, she wondered, take advantage of that ancient custom?

He must be, she reckoned, about thirty-five, and Leora had only just named their wedding day. It was possible. Kerry had seen many beautiful young women in the village as she passed through. And, after all, she mused, Carlos *was* human. He couldn't be occupied at all times with family matters and those of business, and continental men often had a dual morality. They were notoriously prudish when it came to their wives and sisters, but not so with other women.

Kerry made her way slowly up the stairs. If it were true that Roberto was the result of an affair with a village girl, it was surely probable that Leora did not know about it. Or did she? That girl

131

was so difficult to understand.

Kerry stopped outside the door to her room, her fingers frozen over the handle. Now she knew what had troubled her when she first saw the boy; Roberto had been wearing a medallion on a chain, very much like the one that had belonged to Ferdy. The one Kerry had given to Dona Elvira yesterday.

7

From that day onwards Kerry stayed in her room later than on the previous days, allowing Leora time to go to the church, and so avoid any awkwardness that might ensue.

Most of the time Luis was available to keep her company, and although Kerry was in one way glad of that, in another she was not; Carlos frowned and looked generally displeased when he saw them together, and when he spoke to either of them he was no more than coldly polite. Not that Kerry cared for her own sake; she just did not want to cause ill-feeling between the brothers. Luis would have to remain here long after she had gone.

Nevertheless Kerry spent her days being shown over the valley by Luis. They invariably travelled on horseback and Kerry was surprised at how much there was to see. Her days were filled with activity, and some of her time was spent with Dona Elvira. Dinner invariably included them all, and after dinner the evening was spent either talking or playing cards, and occasionally watching the television.

In spite of such a leisurely life, the week was flying past. On Sunday Kerry remained at the *casa* while the others attended the little church in the village. Before she had hardly realised it a whole week had passed and a new one was beginning. During her time at Casa Ramiros Kerry had seen so little of Carlos, and then only in the company of the others, that she was beginning to suspect that he was avoiding her. Since their initial clash he had remained at the *casa*, or at least in the valley, and obviously he was not prepared to accept her as easily as his mother had done.

On the occasions she spent with Dona Elvira, she was surprised to find her attending to much of the administration of the estate, which was, she discovered, very extensive. The Ramiros family ran what appeared to be a little welfare state within the valley. As Dona Elvira had said, 'These people have been loyal to us for centuries, Kerry. They deserve our loyalty in return.'

To Kerry's relief their conversation always remained mainly on a general note and Dona Elvira displayed none of the morbid wish to exchange anecdotes about her dead son, as Kerry had dreaded she might.

But it was not until Dona Elvira had said, the previous afternoon, 'I need a secretary,' that Kerry recalled what Leora had said to her a few days ago. 'I did have a very efficient one but she left just before Fernando died, and I haven't been able to get one since. It isn't easy to find someone to live and work out here.' She hesitated and Kerry knew what would come next as the woman looked at her speculatively. 'I don't suppose you would consider staying on to help me. There would be very little work to trouble you.'

Kerry smiled to herself. Dona Elvira was going about it in a very devious way, but Kerry knew she was being invited to remain indefinitely, as Leora had warned her she would. She wondered what Carlos would think to that idea!

'But I know nothing about secretarial matters,' she pointed out.

'You do not need to know anything. You will soon learn, and as I have said, there is very little to do.'

'I'm sorry,' Kerry answered gently, 'but I have a family in England, and a career that I enjoy very much. There isn't much point in my staying here. It may seem dreadful to you, but I want the opportunity of meeting someone else. I'm not made of the stuff to stay faithful to a memory.'

Dona Elvira looked up at her, her eyes narrowing slightly. 'Do you think any woman is?'

Kerry was slightly taken aback and then she answered, rather hesitantly, 'I'm not sure.'

Dona Elvira drummed her fingers on the arm of her chair and stared ahead. 'I wonder . . . ' she murmured. Then she looked up at Kerry again as if assessing her. 'If you want to stay, there is no need for me to think up a silly excuse for you. We will look after you. You are accepted here now, as one of us.'

Kerry smiled. 'Thank you. I'm honoured, but what I said before still stands.'

'Well, if you do go, don't expect to be welcomed back every time you want a free holiday. If you stay, you stay, and if you go you do not come back.'

'Yes, I understand,' said Kerry bleakly. Why did they have to behave in such an uncompromising way? she asked herself. Why couldn't the ties remain without a risk of being strangled by them?

When Kerry wandered into the garden the following morning she remembered clearly her conversation with Dona Elvira the previous day. She recalled, too, the way in which Carlos remained polite and distant to her and it still rankled, as much as his anger had done. His indifference was like an unhealed sore. Kerry thought the time for leaving was drawing near, and somehow it saddened her.

The sun was climbing rapidly in a still cloudless sky and three elderly men, their straw hats tipped over their eyes, were tending the garden. Each bade her a polite 'Buenas dias' before returning to their work, and Kerry was glad of an opportunity to sit in the shade and read the paperback novel she had started on the plane.

But still as the air was, there was activity to distract her; bees were buzzing round the roses, the fountain was hissing gently, and there was the chip-chip-chip of the gardeners' hoes and the continual flight of the swallows through the orange and lemon trees. After a while Kerry closed her book, sat back and closed her eyes.

Only moments later her eyelids

fluttered open at the sound of footsteps approaching. She sat up sharply and found herself squinting against the sun at the man who stood before her. He didn't look at all business-like today. He was wearing a casual lightweight sweater and a pair of linen slacks. But to Kerry he still looked unapproach- able, which was a crazy way to feel, for both Ferdy and Luis were extremely easy to get on with, as was, for that matter, their mother who had seemed alarming at first.

He sat down beside her so she did not have to look up any longer. It was far less tense to have him on a level with her.

'I saw you from the window of my office. I hope I didn't disturb you.'

'Not at all,' she answered stiffly without looking at him. Why can't I be natural with him? she asked herself. 'I hope I didn't disturb *you*.'

To her surprise he smiled. 'No, you did not do that. I was hoping to catch you alone. I have been trying for a week.'

'For a busy man, you're at home quite a lot, aren't you?' she said, unable to keep the challenge out of her voice. The reason she believed him to have stayed at Casa Ramiros had continued to annoy her.

'I do a great deal of work here.' He sat back on the seat. 'Last week I was in Madrid and perhaps next week also. For the moment there is no pressing need for me to be anywhere else but here.'

Because I'm here, she thought to herself.

He began to fumble in his pocket. 'It is so delightful sitting out here with you, I was forgetting my original reason for seeking you out. I wanted to give you this.'

He brought out her engagement ring, about which she had almost forgotten. Certainly she wanted to forget the way she had lost it.

He held it out to her. 'I thought you would want it back.'

She made no move to take it. 'It must

have seemed a childish thing to do.'

'You were upset, and when one is upset anything can happen. It is understandable. I didn't help.' Kerry looked at him in astonishment. His eyes met hers, warm and understanding. She could hardly believe the difference in him.

'Please,' he insisted, 'take it. It is yours.'

At last she took it from him and slipped it automatically onto the finger of her right hand, something he did not miss.

'I *am* no longer engaged,' she pointed out. She felt that an explanation was necessary and yet it irritated her to have to make one. 'I may as well get used to the idea, painful as it is.'

'It is not easy for us to regard you as free.'

'Your mother has asked me to stay here,' she said quickly. 'She probably feels the same way. I think she would like me to stay here for good.'

'And do you intend to?' he asked,

and she sensed he had stiffened slightly.

No one had ever made his dislike of her so patent, and even though she tried not to care, it hurt.

'No, you see I am free, Carlos. How can it be otherwise? I looked forward to being married, and I still want to be married one day, but I cannot marry a dead man.'

He glanced down at her naked left hand, at her long slim fingers with their pearly pink nails. She knew already that their brief *rapport* was over. Perhaps it had never even happened.

'By the way that you speak, it looks very much as if you have someone in mind already.'

Her eyes opened wide in horror. 'Only two months after Ferdy died?' She stood up abruptly. It felt good just to be able to look down on him. 'Luis warned me you didn't have a good opinion of English girls, but I didn't think you would regard my feelings as quite so trifling. It's obvious now you don't think I have any feelings at all!'

Without waiting for any reply or protest he might make she dashed into the house. Ferdy had been easy to know but the rest of his family were totally unfathomable. No wonder he had left home.

In the comparative gloom of the hall with its small shuttered windows and dark furniture, she almost collided with Leora who was looking as cool as usual. Her sleeveless suit was immaculate, her face matt, and there was not one dark hair out of place.

What a well-suited pair, Kerry thought immediately, cool and unruffled at all times, able to handle grief and anger with the utmost dignity. Cold, she thought, cold and mechanical, and yet . . .

Leora looked at Kerry critically. 'Are you all right?' she asked. 'You look a little upset.'

Kerry nodded. She was already regretting this latest outburst, wishing she could remain as cool as Carlos himself. He never needed to lose his temper to make his feelings known.

'Yes, I'm all right. I'm just warm,' she answered, collecting herself quickly.

'We are used to the heat. It gets worse.' She hesitated a moment as Kerry wiped her sticky hands and her brow on a handkerchief. 'I am sorry if you have to spend some time alone, but Luis has had to go out . . . '

Carlos has sent him out, away from my disruptive influence, Kerry thought. My only friend.

' . . . and I am about to visit friends. Dona Elvira has a headache today also.'

'Oh, I am sorry,' answered Kerry, genuinely concerned. 'I'll call in to see her later. But don't concern yourself with me, Leora. I'm enjoying myself and wouldn't want anyone to be inconvenienced on my behalf.'

Leora smiled slightly as if ridiculing the idea that anyone *would*.

'I was going to ask,' Kerry went on quickly, 'if it was all right for me to sunbathe. I know it isn't always the thing to do . . . '

In fact Kerry had only just thought of

it. Up until that moment she hadn't had the desire or the opportunity to sit out in the sun, but she did have the time now and in just a few days, if the weather continued as it was, she would have a lovely honey-coloured tan which would be in great demand by photographers at home. Her fairness luckily had never been a bar to sunbathing. A slight sun tan had the effect of turning her into a real golden girl.

'You may do whatever you wish,' came the reply.

'On the balcony?'

'Of course.' She picked up her bag from the hall table. 'I must go now. I have a lot of people to see today.' She smiled in a way that was sweet for her, although Kerry could not help but be constantly aware of a hard core of dislike for her in Leora. 'Adios, for now.'

Back in her room Kerry gratefully stripped off her clothes, leaving them in a heap on the floor. The windows were open and the shutters closed, making the room deliciously cool. Normally Kerry could take a reasonable amount of heat with no ill effects, but her encounter with Carlos had, as usual, sent her temperature soaring by several degrees.

After she had had a quick, cooling shower, Kerry put on two scraps of material which passed for a bikini and took a towel from the bathroom to cushion the floor of the balcony. Her skin glistened with an anointing of sun oil. The sun, soaking into her skin, had a relaxing effect. She felt calmer now. After a while she turned over and lay face down on the towel, cradling her face on her arms.

The sun beat incessantly on her back and unwillingly she began to think about Carlos and especially the way his eyes had met hers. Her heart gave an involuntary little lurch. She was glad of the sun; the heat was so intense it was almost as if it were purging her of unwelcome thoughts.

Her head came up sharply. There was

a noise somewhere near. She felt completely bemused and wasn't even sure where she was for the moment. Before she could collect her thoughts, she felt herself being seized roughly round the middle and lifted forcibly from the ground. Naturally, as she was half dragged and half carried into the bedroom she screamed.

'Be quiet, you little fool,' said a familiar voice in her ear. 'Are you mad to go to sleep in this heat?'

As he propelled her into the bathroom she was totally unable to stop him. 'Luis!' she gasped, 'Let me go. I didn't mean to fall asleep. I'm not that stupid.'

'Aren't you?'

Before Kerry knew what was happening to her he pushed her under the shower and turned on the cold tap. As the icy water gushed down over her hair and face, and now very tender back, she screamed again, a scream that ended in a shudder.

'Be quiet,' he insisted. 'Do you want

147

to have everyone along here to see you like this?'

'Yes,' she gasped. 'Yes, I do. I want someone to save me from a lunatic who's on the loose and needs locking up again.'

She was answered only by a laugh and at last she opened her eyes. So great was her surprise that she stayed under the shower, quite oblivious to it.

'Carlos, it's you! I was so sure it was Luis. I never thought you would do anything like this! Oh, you're far worse than I thought you were.'

He smiled. 'I'm sorry you think that. Perhaps if I had have been Luis, you would have found this not at all outrageous; amusing perhaps. I'm so sorry you are disappointed.'

'You're mad,' she cried again as her teeth began to chatter. He leaned over and turned off the tap at last. The water dripped down her hair and face as she clasped her arms about her body. She was freezing cold.

He held out a large bath towel.

'Come out now or you will have pneumonia to add to your sunburn, and the doctor will think *he* is crazy.'

'I don't need a doctor! I was just enjoying myself out there, minding my own business. It's you who needs help!'

He smiled. 'We shall see.'

She let out a little scream of vexation. 'You've done this to humiliate me.' She was fighting the pitiful, angry tears which were threatening to pour down her cheeks.

'On the contrary, I did it to save you a painful sunburn, or even worse than that.'

He was still holding the towel and at last she stepped into it. He wrapped it round her and made no attempt to let her go.

'I should think you'd enjoy putting me out of action for a while,' she said sniffing away the little drops of water which were dripping down her nose.

He let her go at last. He was suddenly serious. 'In this country a severe sunburn could put you out of action — as you put it — for good. Nasty as I am, I am not such a blackguard as to want that.'

She refused to be won over so easily although she knew she had cause to be grateful to him. She had acted stupidly yet again, but she still would not admit that his method was right. He had enjoyed pushing her under the cold jet, and even more, he was finding her acute embarrassment amusing.

'You'd best keep covered for a day or two,' he advised as he backed out of the room. 'And,' he added when she followed him, dripping water as she walked, 'the next time you decide to do it, please sunbathe on the roof terrace where you cannot be seen by everyone who comes to the house.' He smiled again. 'You looked very nice, I admit, but I prefer my workers to go about their duties rather than think up excuses to come to the house . . . '

She pulled the towel around her automatically. 'They didn't!'

'Be assured that they did. It was because there was such an influx of people — men — that I came out to investigate the attraction. I don't want it to happen again. Their womenfolk would soon rebel, you see. In Spain we are not used to such attractive sights. It could prove too much . . . '

He was at the door. Kerry felt as if she could throw the table lamp at him. On reflection she decided she liked him much better when he did not try to be nice to her.

'But Leora said . . . ' she began to protest, and then she stopped herself.

'Yes?' he asked, quirking one eyebrow. 'What did Leora say?'

She averted her eyes. 'It was nothing.' She turned away thoughtfully. 'I shall just smooth some cream on my arms and back. I don't think it's too badly burnt. I'm sorry if I upset anyone.'

He opened the door a little wider as he was about to go. 'Personally, I can never understand what it is about the sunshine that makes tourists want to take off their clothes at the first sight of it. I think a smooth white skin is much more attractive.'

Then he was gone, closing the door behind him, leaving Kerry to wonder whether he were angry or just amused.

A smooth white skin, he had said. She ran her finger along her cheek. Was it a compliment? She stiffened. No. Leora had a pale skin. And Leora had said it would be all right for her to sunbathe on the terrace.

Leora must have known the effect it would have on the men who worked in and around the casa, men whose lives had changed little since the time of Ferdinand and Isabella. The bitch, thought Kerry. She did it deliberately, but she wasn't to know she was doing Kerry a kindness. Had she been directed to the terrace on the roof and fell asleep there, no one would have noticed her; she might have been fried to a crisp. Kerry shuddered at the thought of it and then, as she allowed

the towel to drop, she smiled mischie-
vously. She had actually enjoyed having
his arms around her for those brief few
moments.

8

Kerry decided she would not trust Leora's word about anything in the future.

When she was dressed, covered from neck to knee this time, she went along to Dona Elvira's suite and found, somewhat to her surprise, that she was, indeed, suffering from a headache. Dona Elvira had her own personal maid, a hefty unfeminine woman called, incongruously, Desiree.

'Dona Elvira, she is ill,' Desiree informed her in English, but with an accent so thick that Kerry could hardly understand what was said.

At least Leora had not lied about that. Perhaps, Kerry was wondering now, she had misjudged the girl after all. Perhaps it was she, herself, who was mistaken. Leora had been in a hurry; she might have thought Kerry had meant the roof terrace. Kerry wasn't completely convinced, for she was sure Leora would take the opportunity of causing her mischief if she could, but she was certainly willing to give her the benefit of the doubt on this occasion.

'Who is there, Desiree?' asked Dona Elvira from within the suite.

'Senorita Loveday, *dona*. I have just informed her you cannot be disturbed.'

'Nonsense,' came the short reply. 'Come along in, child. I only have a headache; I am not dying.'

Kerry looked at Desiree with uncertainty but the woman simply opened the door wider and shrugged her huge shoulders, saying, 'Senorita Leora instructed me to allow no one in.'

Kerry went slowly into the room, smiling grimly to herself. Leora again. An order like that would only apply to herself. It was hardly likely to stop either Carlos or Luis visiting their mother if they wished to do so.

Inside the sitting-room the shutters were closed and Dona Elvira was coming out of the bedroom. Her face was white and pinched.

'If I'd known you were ill, Dona Elvira, I wouldn't have come,' she said, moving back towards the door. 'I'll leave you to rest and call back later.'

Dona Elvira waved her hand in the air impatiently and sank down into her favourite high-backed chair. Today she did indeed look like an old woman.

'It is nothing. A headache. I slept badly last night. A little company is what I need most. I don't want to be on my own just now. Please stay with me a while.'

'Well, if you're sure . . . '

'Yes, I never say anything unless I am sure.' Kerry could believe it. Dona Elvira laid her head against the back of the chair and closed her eyes. 'Sometimes life is very difficult, Kerry. There are so many pitfalls in it, and as one grows older they increase.'

Kerry watched her carefully. 'Something has happened to upset you.'

She kept her eyes closed, but her lips

curved into a smile. 'It need not concern you.'

'Are you sure it doesn't concern me, Dona Elvira?'

She drew a deep sigh. 'Yes, my dear, I am quite sure.'

It was some time later that Kerry was allowed to leave Dona Elvira. They'd had lunch together, although neither had eaten very much. Kerry was puzzled and a little alarmed at Dona Elvira's lethargy, but the woman made little of it and they spoke of other, general, matters.

Earlier, whilst waiting for her hair to dry, Kerry had written to her mother at last. Rather guiltily she had realised only then that she had forgotten all about the people at home. The trouble was, while she was away, the life she led in London seemed totally unreal. The only reality now, strangely, was the life she was leading in Valparaiso. She had become used to it with surprising ease.

She had written a lengthy letter, which she hoped would satisfy her mother's curiosity, even though Kerry only stated facts and said nothing in detail about the Ramiros family. Indeed there was very little she could say even now; she was still unsure of them.

After leaving Dona Elvira, she went to her room but stayed there only long enough to pop the letter into the pocket of her dress, and then she went outside. No one would miss her if she went to the village. The whole household enjoyed a long siesta, although, when she passed the room Carlos used as an office she could hear him speaking on the telephone. She doubted if he indulged in the siesta habit. Sourly, Kerry thought he must be far too busy running everyone's lives. In any event, no one usually appeared before dinner, which was a late meal at Casa Ramiros.

Kerry decided to make the short journey on foot. It was possible, she knew, to borrow a car from the garage, or have a horse saddled, but she was in no hurry to get there, or to return.

It was the hottest part of the day, and

Kerry was afflicted by the traditional lethargy. As she walked along slowly she kept to the shade of the olive trees which bordered the narrow road, taking care not to step on any of the prickly pears growing in profusion all around. Here and there small green lizards darted in and out of bushes, causing her to step even more carefully.

Ahead of her the village shimmered in the noon-day heat. Only the thousands of olive and almond trees, which surrounded the village and spread almost as far as the sierras themselves, stopped the land from looking arid and sun baked.

Her walk was quite a short one and Kerry passed no one except for a mangy dog who paused to eye her hopefully. It would be easy, she thought, for some passing traveller, finding himself in the valley by a mischance, to think despite its well-kept air that Valparaiso was deserted.

As she entered the village, half a dozen women were washing clothes in the stream that flowed from the sierras and irrigated the valley. Even though there was electricity in the village and the people prospered nowadays enough for the families to enjoy many modern comforts, most of the women preferred the age-old method and the chance to exchange gossip as they went about it.

They stopped their magpie chatter when Kerry approached, eyeing her silently and with curiosity. How different was her bright summer dress to their almost uniform black.

She called out a cheerful '*Buenas tardes*, senoras,' as she passed and they chorused in unison which amused Kerry, '*Buenas tardes*, senorita,' before resuming both their washing and their chatter.

Kerry recalled seeing a general store in the main village square when she had been there before; the type of store to be found in any little village anywhere in the world. It was sure to be the official post office too.

The shutters were just being raised

after the siesta when Kerry arrived. The proprietor took charge of the letters and assured Kerry that they would be on their way that very evening.

She bought an ice lollipop while she was there and went back out into the *plaza*, which seemed a grand name for the square of such a small village. Kerry slipped her sunglasses on again. It was cooler now but the sun still shone and every building without exception looked newly whitewashed and were dazzling to an eye unused to it.

The air was filled with the scent of rosemary which was often used as a cooking fuel. Kerry inhaled deeply of its sweetness and walked across to the stone fountain in the centre of the *plaza*. She sank down on the bottom step which led up to it and ate the lollipop slowly, feeling the spray from the fountain playing on the back of her neck. It made her feel deliciously cool, as if the gentle fingers of a lover were touching her skin. As she sat there, the children of the village were starting to come out to play and their mothers to gossip with each other.

There were two cars in the *plaza* — small ones, which were dusty, of course. It wasn't usual to see many cars in the valley. There were several at the *casa*, but it was so much easier to travel on horseback, or, for most of the villagers, by donkey.

Across the *plaza* a child, playing alone, caught her attention. Kerry's heart jerked beneath her ribs. *Roberto*. She watched him for a moment or two, recalling Leora's agitation at seeing the child at Casa Ramiros the other day, and Dona Elvira's sleepless night. There could be no connection, and yet there was a sickly feeling in the pit of Kerry's stomach. Her supposition, that the child belonged to Carlos, *was* right, she was sure. Why else would the two women be so upset? Which meant that Leora knew too! But did Dona Elvira?

Almost unwillingly Kerry was walking towards him. She smiled brightly when the child became aware of her.

'*Olà*, Roberto.'

The little boy hung his head shyly. He was still wearing the San Fernando medallion. It looked very much like Ferdy's but Kerry was well aware such medallions were far from unique. She stooped down and cradled the medallion in the palm of her hand.

'This is beautiful,' she said slowly in Spanish.

The child beamed. 'San Fernando. The patron saint of Valparaiso.'

'Yes, I recognise it. Where did you get this? Did your mother give it to you? Your father?'

Kerry hated herself for questioning the boy. Whoever was his father, even if it were Carlos, it was none of her business, and she despised herself for even displaying curiosity.

The child just smiled and said nothing, and she wondered if he had understood her. She turned the medallion over and peered at the words engraved on the other side. *Con amor*, and there was a date — six years previously. *With love*, and the date. Kerry stared at it for a moment or two, for there was something familiar about it, and then it came to her in one blinding flash. She straightened up abruptly. The child frowned at the change in her demeanour.

With love, and Ferdy's birthday — his twenty-first birthday.

'*Venga*, senorita,' Roberto invited, moving away.

Kerry went with him, through an archway to a narrow, cobbled *calle*. The houses were built in the customary way, close together, and every balcony was a mass of geraniums which spilled through the iron railings and hung suspended over their heads.

She was still feeling dazed and slightly shocked, trying to work out the meaning of those words. And who could have written them on Ferdy's twenty-first birthday, and why was the child wearing it?

Coincidence, she told herself sternly. Birthdays were not exclusive to one person, and surely she would have noticed the writing before now if it were indeed Ferdy's medallion. And, yet, how could she? He never seemed to take it off, at least not in her company. He always wore that medallion, she recalled.

The answer was, Kerry told herself firmly, that it wasn't Ferdy's medallion at all. The child wasn't even the result of Carlos's indiscretion either. The likeness was uncanny, the more she looked at the child the more likenesses she saw, but he was just a throwback to an earlier generation. But Kerry couldn't quite convince herself.

She followed the child a short way from the square. In front of one of the tall, narrow houses, stood a small cart.

'You live here?' she asked.

He nodded but his mind was on something else entirely. He reached into his cart and drew out what looked like a large piece of modelling clay. He sank down onto the ground and began to work it with quick, clever fingers. In only a matter of seconds he had fashioned a horse, and although it was crude it was extremely good for a child so young.

'That's marvellous, Roberto!' cried Kerry, for the moment forgetting all else. 'You are a clever boy.'

The child beamed with pleasure at such praise, and then suddenly came a sharp summons, 'Roberto, *venga*!'

Roberto snatched back his clay horse and began to run back towards the old woman who had come out of the house. Kerry was just about to say she hoped Roberto wouldn't be scolded on her account, but the words died in her throat as Leora followed Senora Penaro from the house.

'What is he up to?' she asked the old woman. 'Is he all right?' When she saw Kerry her face reddened.

'What are you doing here?' she demanded.

Kerry was completely taken by surprise, first at seeing Leora and then by such a fiercely uttered question.

'Did you follow me on purpose?' she insisted when Kerry didn't answer her previous question.

'No, of course not!' Kerry protested as she found her voice again. 'I came to post some letters and started to speak to Roberto as I was leaving the village.' She stiffened. 'I like children. Surely they've not been forbidden to speak to strangers in this place.'

Some of the tension drained out of Leora then. 'I am sorry. I was just surprised to see you here, Kerry. I hope you don't think I was being rude just now.'

'The surprise was mutual,' answered Kerry dryly.

Leora came into the street and smiled at Senora Penaro, saying, '*Adios*, senora. I will call again but in the meantime I hope that your back will soon be much better.'

'*Con mucho gusto*,' murmured the woman as she took hold of Roberto's hand.

Leora looked down at him and

ruffled his hair. 'Adios, Roberto,' and the child grinned shyly. 'Be a good boy now, and do as you are told.'

Leora then looked at Kerry who wasn't sure what she thought any longer. Surely Leora wouldn't be so amiable towards Roberto if he were Carlos's child. And yet her consternation at seeing her there, outside Senora Penaro's house, was not caused by surprise alone.

Fortunately Kerry didn't have a chance to think about it too much, for Leora said, 'May I offer you a ride back to Casa Ramiros? You must be remarkably hardy to walk here in the full glare of the afternoon sun.'

Kerry was glad to agree, and they walked the short distance to where the car was waiting in the plaza. 'Even a short distance seems a long one in this heat,' she agreed.

'You are not used to it,' answered Leora as she started up the engine.

'No, indeed,' murmured Kerry. 'Where I come from I can walk for miles and

168

still feel fresh when I come home.'

'It sounds very nice,' said Leora turning away from her. 'You will be glad to return soon.'

Kerry laughed, a little wryly at that comment, but made no reply.

As the car set off, Kerry glanced back but Senora Penaro was no longer there, and, quite unconcerned, Roberto was chasing a dog around the fountain.

She sat back in her seat. 'It was a surprise to see you at Senora Penaro's house so soon after she had been to see Dona Elvira . . . ' she ventured, watching Leora carefully.

'It is the custom to make village visits. It is the *dona*'s custom but of course Dona Elvira lately has had no heart to visit. I am doing it for her more and more. We call on everyone but mainly those widowed, ill, and so on. Senora Penaro has not been too well lately.'

An involved explanation, thought Kerry, for one usually so uncommunicative. 'It must be quite a task for her to look after a child like Roberto.'

'Looking after children and grand-children is no hardship in Spain. And Senora Penaro loves Roberto.'

'Did you know Roberto's father?'

Leora turned to stare at Kerry for a moment and then, realising she was in charge of a vehicle, turned back to concentrate on the road ahead.

'Of course. I told you; he is dead.' She passed one hand across her forehead in a weary gesture. 'Please, let us not talk of it any more. They are just one family, and there are so many in the village. I cannot understand why you are so interested.'

Kerry had no answer to that, at least not one she could tell Leora. The car came to a halt outside the gates. Leora took the opportunity of looking at Kerry again.

'I thought you were taking a sun bath today. Isn't that what the English like best about Spain? Isn't that why they put up with our barbaric ways, atro-cious plumbing and even worse food?'

The gate was opened by the old man and Leora tugged at the handbrake and the car shot into the courtyard. Kerry looked at her in amazement, wondering what she had done to deserve such a tirade.

'I don't know about other visitors,' she answered as the car screeched to a stop, 'but I don't regard Spain in such a way.'

Leora stared at her for a moment or two and then she snatched up her handbag from the back seat. 'Again I must ask you to forgive me. I sometimes forget my manners.'

'You're not alone in that,' answered Kerry wearily as she got out of the car. Perhaps, she thought, wedding nerves were already beginning to afflict Leora.

They walked in silence as far as the gate to the garden and then Kerry said, 'Why did you say it was all right for me to sunbathe on my balcony?'

Leora's eyes grew ingenuously wide. 'I said nothing of the kind!'

'But you did!'

'Surely you know you must go on the roof because there the servants would not be able to see you. Our men are unused to seeing women unclothed in public. Only on the beaches of the resorts is it permissable.'

'I realise that now, but I was so sure you'd said . . . '

Leora pushed open the gate. 'You are mistaken. Did you sunbathe on the balcony of your room?'

'Yes, I did.'

'I hope you did not become too much of a spectacle. It is important in these uncertain times to retain the respect of our workers. In Spain women are idealised to a great extent. The men may appear to like to see a woman expose herself but they still prefer a woman to have a little mystique, and be able to admire and respect her.'

Kerry followed her angrily through the garden. Leora had no business to read her a lecture. She *was* certain Leora had told her to sunbathe on the balcony and her denial now could only mean that she had deliberately taken the opportunity to cause mischief. The first Kerry had learned of a roof terrace was when Carlos had told her about it.

'I don't think I was out there long enough to make a spectacle of myself,' Kerry answered, quickly swallowing her anger. Losing her temper with Leora would not solve anything. 'Carlos came and brought me inside.'

Leora stopped on the bottom step of the house and looked at Kerry expressionlessly. 'Carlos, you say.'

Kerry looked away. 'Yes.'

'He must have been furious with you.'

Kerry walked past her. When she reached the top step she paused and turned. 'No, I don't think so, Leora. Anyway, both you and I know very well that Carlos has no right to frown on something as innocent as sunbathing in a perfectly respectable bikini . . . don't we, Leora?'

She didn't wait for a reply. She was

satisfied enough to have astonished
Leora for once.

★   ★   ★

Carlos was alone in the *sala* when
Kerry went down for dinner that
evening. She was still a little embarrassed in his presence, but was very
much aware she was looking her best
tonight. For the first time since coming
to Valparaiso she felt as if she were
Kerry Loveday, the successful photographic model whose face millions of
men admired and as many women tried
to emulate.

Luckily her skin hadn't blistered but
had taken on a light golden hue. With
her hair drawn back away from her face
and her neck, and wearing the emerald
green evening gown that became her so
well, Kerry knew she was worthy of
admiration. What puzzled her was why
she suddenly needed to receive admiration from anyone just now.

When she entered the *sala* she looked

to see if any admiration had appeared in his eyes and at last she realised that this was what she had wanted all the time. *His* admiration. Heaven help me, she thought. The sun must have gone to my head after all.

Although this sudden and shattering awareness threw her into confusion, outwardly she managed to remain calm. And he was as urbane and as distant to her as ever. In fact he seemed positively preoccupied.

He got to his feet as she entered but it was as if he was hardly seeing her. 'For a short while I thought my watch must be wrong.'

'I think it's the others who are a little later than usual.'

She sat down but could not relax. To cover the confusion of her own feelings she lit a cigarette. He had remained standing.

'Would you like an aperitif?' He indicated his own glass of *manzanilla*.

She shook her head and then he sat down again. There was nothing else to say but at least she was glad he hadn't mentioned what had happened this morning.

He lifted his glass but then put it down again. He looked up at her.

'Kerry,' he said thoughtfully.

She looked at him eagerly. 'Yes . . . '

But before he could say any more Luis came hurrying into the *sala*, exclaiming 'Kerry, I have been looking for you all day! Have you been hiding from me?'

She was momentarily diverted but she immediately turned back to Carlos. He was standing up again, for his mother was following Luis into the room, and Kerry realised that whatever Carlos was going to say would now remain unsaid.

Luis came up to her as Carlos greeted his mother, and she tried hard to suppress the unreasonable dismay she was feeling. It was the first time Carlos had not called her Miss Loveday.

'I have been in and out,' she

answered Luis. 'I was in the village for a while.' She glanced at Dona Elvira who appeared to be much recovered although still a little pale and pinched, and was engaged in conversation with her until it was time to go into the dining-room.

Surprisingly it was Leora who did not come down for dinner. 'She has a migraine,' explained Dona Elvira. 'She wishes me to give her apologies to you all for her absence.'

'Leora suffers badly from migraine,' said Carlos who had been unusually silent throughout the meal, although Kerry had been aware of his pensive gaze on her from time to time. 'She has had attacks occasionally for the past few years.'

'Oh, what a pity,' answered Kerry with genuine feeling. It could account for her bad temper earlier. 'I understand it can be very painful. Isn't there anything to be done to help her?'

She looked from Carlos to his mother and it was she who answered. 'Nothing, except rest and quiet.'

'Some years ago,' Carlos added, 'Mama took Leora round Europe in an attempt to find a doctor who could help.' He looked at his mother. 'Isn't that so?'

Dona Elvira murmured an indistinct 'Yes' as she concentrated, with unusual vigour, on her food.

Carlos turned to Kerry again. 'Nothing they prescribed was of any real use, but fortunately it does not affect her too frequently.'

'I'm glad to hear it,' murmured Kerry who was still watching Dona Elvira whose eyes remained downcast. 'I must admit I thought she wasn't quite herself today.'

'You noticed that?' said Dona Elvira in surprise.

Kerry looked at her boldly. 'Yes, she was quite upset when she saw me in the village.'

Dona Elvira did not reply and it was Luis who said,

'She may have been upset to find you

had walked all the way to the village.'

'It wasn't far.'

'But the sun was strong,' answered Carlos, and his tone was mildly amused. 'You must learn to treat the sun with respect, Miss Loveday, or the consequences may be serious.'

He was laughing at her, she knew, and she refused to answer or to look at him. His abrupt changes of mood were as maddening as they were unexpected.

Luis sat back in his chair. His eyes sparkled with amusement too. He twirled his empty wineglass between his fingers.

'I wonder if this is a good time to ask if you would accord me the honour of coming to Granada with me tomorrow.'

Kerry, in normal circumstances, wouldn't have hesitated to agree. She was anxious to see the famous city whilst she was in Andalusia, and suddenly life at Casa Ramiros was becoming a little too enclosed and involved. But she did hesitate. She couldn't help but look at Carlos, waiting for him to voice his disagreement, or perhaps to remind Luis that he had an 'appointment' elsewhere. But his eyes met hers artlessly, and Dona Elvira appeared not to have heard.

'I'd like to visit Granada while I'm here,' she answered guardedly at last.

'Then it's settled,' said Luis. 'Tomorrow we will go.'

Dona Elvira looked up then and pushed her plate away from her. 'In my day no young woman would accompany a young man alone without risking her reputation and her future prospects.'

'You may come along to act as *duena*, Mama,' answered her younger son.

Dona Elvira cast him an amused look and Kerry said brightly, 'Well, living on my own as I do, I imagine my reputation is pretty suspect anyway.'

'No one is concerned any more,' said Dona Elvira sadly. 'Young people think they know best, but it is not so.'

'I should think,' said Kerry thoughtfully, 'that even in the old days, couples intent on being alone together found ways of arranging it, and perhaps, nature being what it is, it ended far more disastrously than if they'd been allowed to be alone in the first place.'

No one said anything. Dona Elvira looked at her but it was as if she wasn't seeing anyone. Carlos looked down at his plate and Luis said in a bright tone, 'Well, if everyone is finished . . . '

They had the customary glass of *oloroso*, followed by coffee, before Carlos excused himself.

'I must make a telephone call,' he explained.

'And I must look in on Leora,' said Dona Elvira, frowning suddenly.

When they had gone Kerry smiled across at Luis as she rested her head on the back of the sofa. She was altogether more relaxed now. Luis never caused her to feel uncomfortable in the slightest degree.

'Carlos is away on business tomorrow,' he said, refilling her coffee cup. 'He has not been here for such a long time at once for many years. I was beginning to think he'd retired! Tomorrow is a good opportunity to go out for the day.'

'It sounds wonderful, Luis,' she admitted. 'I did want to see Granada whilst I was here.'

'I warn you; it can be very romantic.'

She laughed. 'Consider me warned, Luis, and you must remember you are engaged; that way we can both enjoy ourselves.'

'Sofia trusts me implicitly,' he boasted.

Kerry laughed again as she sat up to drink her coffee.

'Any woman who trusts a man is a fool.'

He appeared to be dismayed. 'Didn't you trust Ferdy?'

'Of course,' she answered softly. 'He was the one man I could have trusted with a roomful of beauty queens.'

He was looking at her pitying now.

'Poor Kerry,' he murmured.

She looked at him sharply. '*What* did you say?'

He smiled in a way that made him look mature. 'If an old man of a hundred kissed Sofia's hand, flattered her and impressed her, I would be jealous. Love is always like that, Kerry. Didn't you know? Love is jealousy. It is never easy.'

There was no teasing in his tone, no amusement in his voice. Kerry looked away from him. 'Do you know a boy called Roberto who lives in the village?' she asked abruptly.

He frowned for a moment or two. 'I know Roberto Sanchez who sometimes looks after the horses, but he is not reliable. He is very lazy. Sometimes he goes away for days and cannot be found.'

Kerry shook her head impatiently. 'No, this Roberto is a small boy — about four or five years old. He lives with Senora Penaro.'

His face cleared. 'Oh yes, I know who

you mean now. He is the senora's grandchild.'

Kerry sat up straight. 'Grandchild? But Leora didn't say that. She said Senora Penaro looked after him . . . because she had no children of her own.'

Luis laughed. 'You are mistaken, I'm sure. I recall Roberto's mother very well.' He rolled his eyes expressively and for once Kerry was unable to respond to his teasing. 'She fancied herself as a singer, and of course village life became too much of a restriction, so she went to Madrid to seek her fortune.'

Kerry stirred her coffee thoughtfully. It was cold but she hardly noticed that.

'I don't know if she found it,' he added with a laugh, 'but Senora Penaro returned from Madrid one day with the child.'

'Leora, I'm sure, said the parents were dead.'

'That is also possible. But I have told you as much as I know about it.'

Kerry said nothing. Two stories

— Leora's and Luis' — which one was true? Neither, in all probability. It was certain Luis did not suspect the child was his brother's.

His smile faded. 'Why did you ask?'

She looked up at him artlessly. 'Just idle curiosity. Leora visited the family today and I met her there.'

He nodded. 'She visits the old and the sick as my mother has done for many years. Leora is already the *dona* here. Since Ferdy died my mother has been glad to let her. She has heart to do very little,' he added sadly.

Kerry nodded slowly. It was true; Leora was as much in love with the position she would have when she married as with the man she was to marry. Perhaps even more so.

She looked at Luis, her thoughts still a jumble that made no sense.

'You look tired,' he said perceptively. 'You and Carlos have had a disagreement again — no?'

She smiled slightly. 'Not exactly. What made you think so?'

'The way you are oh-so-polite with one another. You are both normally warm human beings. It is quite amusing to watch you two together.'

He laughed and she could not respond.

'Shall we have a stroll around the garden,' Luis suggested. 'And then early to bed so we can have an early start in the morning.'

Kerry got to her feet slowly and smiled with pleasure.

'That's a very good idea.'

She took his arm and walked out with him to the garden. What did it matter if Senora Penaro's daughter had borne Carlos a child, and proud Leora attempted to cover up the circumstances? In little more than another week she would be back in London and it wouldn't matter at all.

9

The maid awoke Kerry with breakfast the next morning. 'Senor Ramiros will meet you at the car, senorita,' the girl informed her, 'in three quarters of an hour.'

When the shutters were opened she stretched lazily before getting out of bed. With the feel of the sun on her face, it was a delightful way to start the day. A whole day away from Valparaiso was ahead of her. Kerry hadn't realised until that moment how much she was looking forward to it. A day out with Luis; Luis who could flirt and charm, and yet not demand to be taken seriously. Happy, easy-going, even-tempered Luis.

No one was around when she went downstairs and Kerry wondered if Leora had recovered from her migraine and if Carlos had left yet on his business trip. It was odd the way he had the habit of creeping into her thoughts so often. Carlos with his maddening reserve, icy flashes of temper, and occasionally, fleeting glimpses of warmth and understanding.

She let herself out of the garden and immediately saw the car, newly washed and waiting in the courtyard. As she approached Pablo, the mechanic, came out of the garage, wiping his hands on an oily rag.

'*Buenas dias*, senorita,' he greeted her.

'*Buenas dias*,' she responded but before she could ask if Luis had come down yet the gate behind her opened and she turned round. Her expectant smile faded when she saw that it was Carlos who came into the courtyard and not Luis. She groaned inwardly and whipped off her sunglasses just in case the light was playing tricks on her. But it was, indeed, Carlos; unconsciously she had dreaded meeting him this morning.

'Ah, good morning, Kerry,' he greeted her. 'You are up bright and early. You must really be looking forward to your trip to Granada.'

He sauntered towards her and her eyes narrowed fractionally. She distrusted his tone. And, she suddenly realised, he looked somehow different. She watched him carefully. He was wearing a pair of casual slacks, a lightweight sweater and he carried a jacket over his arm; clothes, she knew at last, that Carlos, of all people, would not wear for a business trip.

'Have you seen Luis around the house?' she asked, struggling to keep her voice even. 'I'm afraid he might have slept in despite all his good intentions.'

'Not Luis,' he answered, stopping in front of her. Only then did she realise she had backed up to the car, almost defensively. 'He left here, let me see — about half an hour ago.' Kerry stared at him in disbelief and he smiled. 'A sudden matter of business. It was very urgent and quite impossible to postpone. He asks you to accept his apologies . . . '

'Oh, well,' she answered, not hiding her disappointment very well, 'it can't be helped.'

Somewhere in the back of her mind lurked a strong suspicion that Carlos had something to do with this sudden call away from home.

' . . . he was most disappointed, as you can imagine, and I assured him that you at least would go.'

She looked at him sharply as he opened the car door. 'If you will permit me . . . '

'You!' She was suddenly panic-stricken. She looked away. 'But you too were going . . . '

'It wasn't of so much importance. It has been postponed until another day.'

'Oh, I don't want you to do that, Carlos,' she said quickly, breathlessly. He was one of the few men she had to look up to when she spoke. 'It isn't as if it's of real importance, just a sightseeing trip. I can easily go on another day.'

His eyes were laughing at her but his expression remained grave. 'It is of importance to me. After all, since you arrived, everyone else has been honoured by your company — except me.'

She wondered if he were being sarcastic, but decided that sarcasm was definitely not one of his faults. Suddenly she realised why he had accepted Luis's invitation to her so calmly last night; Carlos had intended to take her himself.

He knew then he was going to send his brother away on some contrived excuse, and she felt anger prickle inside her. He must, she thought, really consider me a danger to his brother's moral welfare if he is willing to suffer my company himself for the day. For a man who had fathered a natural child it was sheer impudence, and Kerry seethed silently.

But, whatever she thought, she could say nothing. She flung her sweater into the back of the car, her lips pursed into an angry line.

'Unless, of course,' he added as she slipped into the passenger seat, 'you really don't want my company.'

Her lips remained stiff but she managed to force a smile to them. 'I do want to see Granada.'

He closed the car with a sharp click. 'And so you shall.'

Kerry stared ahead. He started the engine but made no attempt to move off.

'You know,' he said thoughtfully, 'I can't help but feel you can't forgive me.'

She looked at him sharply. 'For what?'

His eyes widened slightly. 'For yesterday. What else?'

She relaxed and managed even to smile. 'I assure you, you are wrong, I appreciate what you did.'

He smiled too. 'Good. I am delighted to hear you say so. The matter has worried me a little. As long as you still do not believe I tried to humiliate you.'

'Did I say that?' She felt more than a

little uncomfortable. 'It must have been in momentary anger.'

'Yes, you were very angry.'

He's laughing at me again, she thought. Why can't I join him and laugh at myself?

'Now we can go,' he said brightly as he disengaged the handbrake.

He nodded to Pablo to open the gate and Kerry turned away to look out of the side window. It was going to be a long day.

★   ★   ★

It was early afternoon before Granada came into sight, mainly because the state of the roads precluded swift travel, and also because they had lingered over, firstly, a pre-lunch aperitif and the *tapas* — a selection of tasty hors d'oeuvres — which was served with it, and then what did prove to be a very good lunch indeed.

The restaurant was not on the main road and was quite isolated. There was no outward sign to show that it was a place open for business, but the food was excellent. Carlos chose carefully from the menu, a meal to suit Kerry and to show her the best of local cuisine. They had *gazpacho* — the famous cold vegetable soup which was never as delicious as this before, followed by *paella* — thick with prawns and other seafood still in the shell, and *polio andaluz* — chicken that was spicy to the palate, and finally, fresh peaches the size of grapefruits.

Every dish pleased the tongue and, surrounded by orange and lemon trees and the distant sierras, there was a wonderful view to draw Kerry's eyes too throughout the meal.

Now they were approaching Granada itself and apart from the magnificent Sierra Nevada, gigantic, snowcapped and very near, as a backdrop, it did not immediately impress her. They drove into the town, down the Gran Via de Colon, named after Christopher Columbus who left Granada to begin his great voyage of discovery on behalf of Queen Isabella herself.

They drove past the statue of Colombus and up the Sabika Hill, towards the Alhambra itself. And there it stood before her, on top of the hill, huge and formidable against mountains and sky.

When the car was parked, Kerry got out without waiting for him to open the door for her. The car park was filled with coaches and several groups were waiting for their guides.

He took her arm to lead her the short distance to the entrance. From the outside the fortress and palace were unimposing — sheer walls of red-brown stone. No wonder Granada had been the last Moorish settlement to fall to the Spanish rulers, she thought.

They entered the Moorish palace by way of the rooms where official business was once dispensed. All the rooms Carlos led her through had fancy stucco walls and richly carved cedar ceilings. The stucco work was amazingly intricate, almost like lace, but Kerry had to use her imagination to visualise them as they once were, embellished with gold.

Few words were exchanged between them as they walked through the maze of rooms which were linked by courtyards, each more magnificent than the previous one. Carlos spoke only to tell her where they were, and yet, entranced as she was by her surroundings, Kerry was at all times aware that he was close by her side.

He took her arm and led her to the hall where ambassadors were received. It, too, still bore traces of its one time magnificence on its walls and carved cedar wood ceiling.

Kerry walked over to one of the high vaulted windows which gave splendid views over the rest of the city and the Sierra Nevada. 'I can just imagine Lorenzo Ramiros here with Ferdinand and Isabella,' she said as she gazed out. 'I can almost see him walking through the palace when it was still in its glory.'

She knew he was looking at her but she dare not look round at him. 'The Moors built the palace so it would be cool in the summer, with lots of fountains and pools, and cold marble floors. Unfortunately, when it was captured, the Spanish foolishly spoiled much of the beauty. It was too ornate — to them it was ungodly — so they whitened all the walls.'

She turned to him then. 'What a pity. I should have liked to have seen it then even though it is still marvellous, like a fairytale palace.' She laughed. 'An Arabian Nights palace.'

He took her arm again. 'Come, I will show you what is commonly known as the harem. You will be interested to see that, I'm sure.'

'Is it really?' she asked, looking at him. She wondered if he were having a joke with her.

'It was where the ruler lived with his wives and concubines and children. Most people like to think of it in a less mundane way.'

They strolled back into the sunshine, into the Court of Lions, so called because in its centre stood twelve stone lions supporting a circular fountain.

Automatically she slipped her arm into his as they walked through it, something she would have considered incredible only yesterday, yet today it was the most natural thing in the world. It was part of the magic of this unique place.

'This is the centre of the ruler's private apartments,' he told her when they reached the fountain and the lions.

Her eyes grew bright as she looked up at him. 'Perhaps the wives and concubines walked in here with the ruler just as we are doing now.'

He looked down at her and smiled, and her heart jerked unevenly. 'It is entirely possible.'

Suddenly breathless she began to walk away. 'I'd like a better view over here.' She walked quickly to the far side of the courtyard without waiting to see if he was following, but he was at her side in seconds.

'Look,' she said, keeping her eyes on the opposite side of the courtyard. 'That archway over there; the columns are just like stalactites — dozens of them. Lace stalactites, cascading down to the ground!'

'Come along,' he said suddenly, 'I'll show you something.'

He took her to the bathing apartments, with their tiled alcoves where the Moors rested after their ritual ablutions. Kerry gazed up at the balconies above.

'Probably musicians played there,' Carlos explained.

'And dancing girls danced . . . '

'That is probable too.'

She shivered suddenly. Her shirt was thin and the building was successfully cool, especially in here. The cold from the stone floors struck through her thin sandals too.

'It is cool in here,' she murmured, and he put his arm around her shoulders.

She looked up at him, almost fearfully when she felt his arm around her, and he smiled down at her. 'Let's get into the sun again.'

She slipped away from his enfolding arm and he walked a few steps ahead of her. They walked past the patio garden of Lindaraxa, unexpectedly green and shady with its profusion of cypresses.

'I expect to see a Moorish potentate any minute now,' she admitted as they strolled along a sun-speckled open gallery. 'Everywhere we go we come upon something entirely unexpected.'

'Well, it wasn't all completed at one time. Each part had a different designer, commissioned by a different ruler.'

He leaned back against the low balustrade and gazed at her as she looked out at the white houses on the hill beyond.

'It's incredibly lovely,' she murmured, almost to herself.

'You're impressed?'

She looked at him earnestly. 'How

could I not be? I've never been to a place that's so out of this world. Even from looking at the outside you can't imagine how ornate it is in here. The palace has a magic all of its own. I can't believe the twentieth century is just outside.'

'I'm glad you're impressed.'

A group of tourists came trooping along the arcade led by their guide, and Kerry and her companion were silent until the crowd had passed. Kerry rubbed her hand absently along the rough plasterwork of the walls.

'They were such barbarians,' she said, 'and yet their building is so fantastic. They had this very great feeling for beauty. The two aspects of nature don't go together.'

'They weren't barbarians, Kerry. They were a highly civilised people. Under the Moorish rule Arab, Christian and Jew lived peaceably together, each contributing their own particular skill to the community. But after the Spanish conquest it was decreed that all the

Moors who wished to remain must be Catholics, and the Jews were expelled without even the choice. Most of the Moors left too rather than abandon the faith. Isabella appointed Torquemada to ensure everyone else followed the faith.'

'The Inquisition,' she murmured, shuddering slightly. There seemed no place to talk of such a thing when the sun shone warmly on the arcades and courtyards of the Alhambra.

'The victims were burned at the stake because the church forbade the shedding of blood. So you see,' he added quietly, 'it wasn't the Moors who were the barbarians. We are an intolerant people but we are slowly learning to be more tolerant.' She looked at him and he held her eyes. 'We just need more time.'

Suddenly she smiled. 'There isn't one of us who couldn't do with being less intolerant.'

In effect she realised they were apologising to each other, and it made her incredibly happy. She drew in a deep breath of contentment and looked away from him at last. The old animosity was gone for ever.

'Is that Sacro Monte over there?' she asked, suppressing a sudden excitement inside her.

He glanced behind him at the hill with its little houses and its cave dwellings, now serviced with sophisticated amenities like electricity and telephone.

'Yes, that is Sacro Monte, but don't ask me to take you to see the gypsies who live there, *querida*, because I shall refuse.'

A light died out of her eyes. She looked at him in dismay. She thought he could refuse her nothing today. 'Oh, why not, Carlos?'

He got to his feet at last. 'Because they are not the real flamenco gypsies. They only want money from the tourists, and if you leave Sacro Monte with your wallet and watch it is a very lucky day. But if you want to see the real dancers I will take you later today.'

Her face relaxed into a smile. 'You're a marvellous guide, Carlos.'

He put his arm around her shoulders without pulling her close, and yet she was aware of him again, his strength, his masculinity. Her smile faded. He wasn't smiling either. He looked into her eyes and the moment was fraught with tension, and then a small group of schoolchildren broke into the silence with their chatter and laughter, and the scolding voice of their teacher.

Carlos relaxed his hold on her and she looked away at last. He thrust his hands into the pockets of his slacks.

'I'll show you some of the gardens, buy you a drink and still have time to take you to pay your respects to Ferdinand and Isabella themselves.'

His tone was brusque and his voice rather thick. When Kerry looked at him again she was composed once more.

'That's a splendid idea, Carlos. Let's go now.'

10

Kerry blinked against the brightness of the sun. After the gloom of the Royal Chapel it was doubly dazzling. They emerged from the quiet chapel, adjacent to the cathedral, into the incongruous bustle of the Gran Via.

The sight of the chapel, where Ferdinand and Isabella lie beneath marble effigies, together with their daughter and son-in-law, behind an iron *reja* — the wrought iron screen which Spanish artists are so adept at making — was a sobering one. As they came out into the main street, Kerry glanced up at him and smiled.

'Awe inspiring, isn't it?'

'It was meant to be,' he answered. 'Their grandson built the chapel as a fitting resting place.'

'It's odd their daughter should have been mad. I wonder what made a handsome man like Philip want to marry her.' She grinned and put her head to one side pensively. 'Do you think it was because she was a princess?'

He looked at her gravely. 'It is generally believed that, although she had always been eccentric, she only became finally mad after her husband died. When he died she refused to have him buried and travelled around the country with his coffin.'

She couldn't meet his eyes. She walked away from him, along the street. The sun had lost much of its power, but it had stamped its glory on the sky by flaming it blood red against purple.

'I think it's quite a good idea to give people descriptive names like they used to do,' she said in a bright voice when he had caught up with her. She looked at him quickly and away again. 'Everyone knows what to expect before they even meet them.'

'It can be a disadvantage too;

mistakes can be made and wrong labels given.'

She paused and smiled at him. They were standing on the pavement again, being jostled from time to time by people passing by.

'Then it's just as well we don't do it any more.'

He took her arm to guide her across the busy road.

'We have a little walking to do before we reach the place where we eat. Do you mind?'

She tucked her arm into his. 'I'm enjoying every moment of the day. I don't ever want it to end. I feel as if it's my birthday!'

He looked amused, but pleased too, and Kerry had spoken no less than the truth.

'I wonder if Pedro the Cruel really was a cruel man,' she murmured, harking back to their previous conversation.

'Probably not all the time.'

'In England there was once a king

called Ethelred the Unready. It was a name that always conjured up the most ridiculous pictures in my mind.'

They were now walking through the steep, narrow cobbled streets of the Albaicin, the old quarter, virtually unchanged for centuries. The houses were built so close together that now and again Carlos had to stoop to prevent himself knocking his head on the jutting eaves of one of them.

'We had a title for most of our kings and queens,' he told her. 'We've had rulers who were cruel, bewitched, even desired.'

His eyes held hers until she looked away at last. 'You seem very interested in our history. Do you know anything about it?'

She smiled wryly. 'Very little. I had enough trouble contending with English history when I was at school.'

'I thought perhaps Fernando might have talked about it to you. He was quite a historian in his own little way. He once wanted to become a teacher.'

Kerry looked at him. 'I never knew that. Why didn't he do it?'

It was his turn to smile. 'My father objected very strongly; it was not a fitting profession for his son.'

'So,' said Kerry lightly, 'he became an artist instead, a far less fitting profession.'

There was a moment's silence between them before he said, a little heavily, 'Kerry, contrary to your firm belief, I did not force Fernando to choose between his home and his career. Believe me, his leaving was sudden and a great surprise to me.'

Her step faltered and she looked at him steadily before going on her way again.

'I wonder,' she mused, abruptly changing the subject, 'what we would be called if we were still given nicknames.'

'Carlos the Tyrant,' he said in all seriousness, 'or perhaps Carlos the Terrible.'

She stopped walking and began to laugh. 'No, not that.'

'I'm relieved.' His eyes held hers. 'For you there would be no problem in finding a suitable name — Kerry the Beautiful.'

She stared at him in disbelief and then she felt her cheeks begin to turn crimson. The conversation was no longer amusing. Abruptly she began to walk on, up a steep flight of steps flanked by little houses built into the hillside amidst cactus and aloes. His words were ringing in her ears.

He followed her quickly, taking three steps at a time, and caught her arm. He swung her round to face him.

'I'm sorry; you're embarrassed.'

She swallowed hard. 'No, Carlos. I'm extremely flattered.'

'Surely it's not the first time you have been complimented in this way.'

'No,' she murmured.

They had passed through the oldest part of the town and the houses in this street were larger and more modern. Carlos pushed open an iron gate behind Kerry.

'We are here,' he said, slipping on his jacket. For the first time she was seeing him uneasy.

She preceded him into a cool patio with its central fountain surrounded by cypresses. The birds were singing in the trees although dusk was rapidly falling now, and Kerry inhaled the air deeply, contentedly. Granada may have cast a weird spell over her but she did not want it to break. When she turned he was looking at her. His face was in shadow so she had no way of knowing what he was thinking, but involuntarily she shivered.

He came forward then and draped her woollen jacket around her shoulders. She stiffened beneath his touch; he could not help but be aware of it and yet instead of letting her go his fingers dug deeper into her flesh.

She could feel the warmth of his breath on her neck and it was like a caress.

'Kerry . . .'

She twisted round, looking into his

face questioningly. His eyes held hers for a few moments but he was the first to look away.

He took her hand and said softly, 'Let's go inside. It's getting late.'

★   ★   ★

The moon was just a thin sliver of silver but it shone down brightly to illuminate the bare landscape. The sky was clear and a million stars sparkled in the heavens. The only sound to be heard inside the car was the soft thrum of the engine.

Kerry snuggled into her jacket although the night was still warm. She glanced at the profile of the man who sat beside her. He, Luis and Ferdy were unmistakably brothers, and yet in so many ways they were unalike.

Kerry knew the day that was now almost over would remain in her memory for ever. Every moment of it would be etched in her mind to be remembered with pleasure in days to come. It had been a day of simple pleasures, but the beauty and grandeur that was Granada could never be forgotten, nor would she forget the man who made it so memorable for her, for she was without doubt now — he had cast the spell.

She glanced at him again. Unbelievably and stealthily he had crept into her heart. There was no use in denying it; no one save herself would ever know of it. Love was never viable until it was returned, and that was just a hopeless dream. As her companion today he had been perfect, but if he were ever to guess her secret longings he would despise her.

They had turned off the main road now. Valparaiso lay ahead, ghostly in the moonlight against the darkened sky.

'Did you enjoy the flamenco dancing?' he asked, breaking the long silence between them.

'Very much,' she answered in a voice only just above a whisper.

The feet, hands and voices of the

dancers had interpreted the insistent beat of the music in such a way as to mesmerise the audience. The stamping, clapping and clicking of castanets was hypnotic and Kerry could sense what was almost hysteria in the dancers as the music moved towards the frenetic climax. Kerry had been very moved by the display.

And as the dancers moved with abandoned energy, their proud and disdainful faces glistening with sweat, and the fingers of the guitar players flew over the strings, Kerry had sat forward in her seat, becoming almost as hypnotically entranced as the dancers themselves. Everyone was intently watching them and then, suddenly, she was aware that Carlos had reached out across the table and had covered her hand with his. That was the most marvellous moment of all, and her hand had remained tightly imprisoned in his until the time came for them to go; too soon, much too soon.

The car jerked to a standstill and he

turned to smile at her. 'Well, here we are,' he said unnecessarily.

'So we are,' she answered. 'I wish I could say I was glad.' She hesitated a moment. 'It really has been a marvellous day, mainly because you made it so. I'll never forget it, and . . . ' She hesitated again. 'I'm glad we're friends, Carlos.'

He leaned over and cupped her face in his hands, kissing her lightly on the lips. She closed her eyes, resisting the impulse to return the kiss.

'I'm glad you made Fernando happy,' he said as he drew away.

She stared at him until he got out of the car to come round to open the door for her.

'Do you mind going in alone? I have to speak to Pablo for a few minutes.'

She smiled brightly. 'Of course I don't mind.'

But she did mind. She wanted to stretch out this enchanting day for as long as she could make it last. She moved away from the car and when she

215

was halfway across the courtyard she stopped and turned. He was still standing where she had left him.

'Good night,' she whispered, 'and thank you again for today.'

'It was a pleasure, *carina*,' he answered softly. '*Buenas noches*. Sleep well.'

Kerry slipped into the patio garden without looking back again, but she had the feeling he was watching her, perhaps feeling as bemused as she. Lights were still on in the house and the air was very still. Nearby, Kerry could hear the low murmur of voices but she had no intention of joining them in the *sala*. The last thing Kerry wanted was company just now. Her emotions were still raw, her feelings too new even for her to understand them properly. She only knew she felt quite differently towards him, wonderfully different.

Kerry soaked herself in the bath for a long time. Her mind dreamily relived the day's events, lingering over that brief kiss; a kiss he would have bestowed on his sister. It was useless, she knew, putting any other construction on it. Still, it had been a kiss . . .

She slipped her nightdress over her head and surveyed herself in the mirror without really seeing anything at all. She'd been so sure she would love again after Ferdy — that had never been in doubt — but the problem was, could she fall in love yet again? Were her feelings so shallow and fleeting? Or could it be she had never really been in love with Ferdy?

Still pensive, she sank down in front of the dressing table and began to pull the pins out of her hair which tumbled past her shoulders in a cascade of pure gold. Both inwardly and outwardly she was restless, and although it had been a long and tiring day, Kerry had never felt less like sleeping.

The maid had left the shutters open and the curtains were hardly moved by the still air. Kerry slipped on her dressing gown and a pair of backless mules and walked out onto the balcony. The scent of roses was strong. It drifted from a thousand blooms in the garden below.

The same sliver of moon that had shone over Granada hung suspended over the valley too. Downstairs the lights had been extinguished except for one in the hall, and no longer could the sound of voices be heard. The birds were gone for the night and the silence was broken only by the recurrent chirping of the ever invisible cicadas.

'How can I bear to leave here now?' she asked herself as the tears came unbidden to her eyes. 'How can I leave without knowing what I really feel for him?'

She brushed the tears away with an impatient hand and was about to go back inside to await the sleep that would be long in coming, when she caught sight of a movement at the far side of the garden.

Kerry was frozen into immobility, and then, when she realised someone was out there, she said softly, 'Luis.' There was no reply. 'Carlos, is that you?'

Still there was no reply. She hesitated only a moment or two and then hurried down the stairs. Her feet were silent on the marble floors. The only sound to be heard was the swishing of her dressing gown against her ankles as she walked.

She came out into the garden and stopped near the fountain, which was now silenced for the night. She glanced around, peering through the darkness, but could see no one. A tree waving, she told herself, although there wasn't the slightest breeze tonight.

Feeling a little foolish, questioning her own motives for coming, she began to walk back to the house. And then she started violently at the sound of a footstep behind her.

'Kerry!'

She whirled round and saw him coming towards her.

'I thought I saw someone when I was on the balcony. I wondered who it was.'

A look of pain crossed his face and it alarmed her. 'Go back to your room, Kerry. You shouldn't be out here. Please go back inside.'

She frowned. 'Is something troubling you?'

He continued to stare at her. It was almost as if he was looking through her. Then he turned away.

Kerry was beginning to feel alarmed. 'Carlos, please tell me what is troubling you.'

'You are.'

'Me? But I thought . . . '

He took her arm and she was too startled to resist even when he pro-pelled her towards a clump of bushes. He drew her into his arms and looked down at her for a long moment.

'You wanted to know what was troubling me? I'll show you.'

He began to kiss her. His lips forced hers apart, his arms drew her closer against him. At first Kerry made a token resistance but it was soon quelled by the intensity of his kiss and by the depth of her own response. At last she had no doubts.

'That is what was troubling me,' he said when he drew away at last. His voice was harsh and Kerry was trembling at the unexpectedness of what had happened between them, that and her own reaction. 'I've been fighting against the desire to take you in my arms since the first day I set eyes on you.'

'What fools we must be,' she said in a shaky voice, laying her head on his shoulder. 'We've wasted so much time fighting each other. I feel, too, that this has been inevitable from the day we met.'

He held her close against his heart and kissed her hair. 'We were not fighting each other, *querida*, but our feelings for each other.'

'You're right, I suppose,' she sighed, snuggling against him.

'This is the first time I've lost a struggle of any kind.'

She gave a shaky laugh. 'I can believe that. It's unlike me too. I never exchanged a cross word with Ferdy the whole time I knew him.'

He held her away from him. 'Then you cannot have loved him. What you felt for Fernando was not the love of a woman for the man she is to marry. You were good friends, no more than that.'

'I see it now, but it was a love of a kind. And now I love you. I'm a very lucky girl.'

He kissed her again and Kerry felt gloriously alive in his arms.

'We both knew today, didn't we, *carina*? There was no denying our feelings after today.'

She sighed happily as he held her tightly. 'Luis warned me Granada was romantic. I should have heeded his warning.'

'It is not Granada; this would have happened anyway. Our only defence would have been for me to leave here the day you arrived and not return until you had left, which was impossible.' He kissed her briefly again. 'Even so, some things are fated. We would have met anyway.'

'I've never believed that until now.'

'I have always believed it,' he murmured against her hair. 'I'm also very much aware that fate can also be cruel.' She looked at him questioningly. 'This is the first time I have ever let anything interfere with my duty to my family.'

She drew away from him slowly and unwillingly he released her. 'What has this to do with duty?'

A fleeting look of pain crossed his face and she grew afraid. 'Have you forgotten?' he asked softly. 'I am to marry Leora soon.'

She put one hand on his arm. 'Then you must tell her how we feel. You can't marry Leora now. You don't love her! I know it!'

He took her hand and led her to a seat which was standing against a wall. No one could possibly see them there in the dark, with trees all around.

He kept her hand tightly imprisoned

in his. 'Leora and I are very fond of each other. We grew up knowing we would be married one day. The decision was not made by us. There is no question of us not marrying. Only if Leora herself wished the agreement to be cancelled would I gladly free her, but she wants to marry me, and our wedding was the wish of her father and mine. It is our duty to carry out that wish. It is a matter of honour.'

'It's feudal, wasteful and stupid!' Kerry cried in a harsh whisper.

He put his finger against her lips. 'It is our custom, *querida*. I am the head of this family now. If I refused to marry Leora I would not only disgrace my family but I would lose the respect of everyone who knows us. That would not be a happy beginning for us.'

She shook her head. 'I don't care about other people's respect. I love you and I know you love me. How can you marry a woman you don't love?'

'Marriage to Leora will not be unpleasant,' he said quietly. 'Many a successful marriage has been based on less. The marriages of my sisters were arranged before they were hardly out of the cradle, and they are both very happy.'

Kerry stared unseeingly ahead, into the darkness.

'Only a naive fool would believe that to love and be loved in return was all that was necessary to make a relationship. Forgive me for being naive. You will have ample compensation in the dowry Leora will bring. She'll make you a very rich and influential man. And I was forgetting, too, that when the novelty of being married to a woman you don't love palls you can always find another village girl to revive your jaded palate.'

He stared at her in amazement. 'You think I would treat my wife in such a way?'

'Why not? You'd treat your fiancée like that.'

'I don't know what you're talking about now. We have so little time left to

be together. Let's not spend it quarrel-
ling again.'

He was about to put his arm around
her but she pulled away. 'I'm not the
only one who knows about it, Leora
knows too.'

'Then you, and she, are more
fortunate than I. Perhaps you'd better
explain what this is all about. What did
you mean by 'another village girl'?' She
said nothing. Kerry just bit her lip. 'I
mean to have an explanation,' he
warned her, 'but before you make it, I'd
better tell you that the girls in Spanish
villages have a stricter upbringing than
those of other families. Their honour is
the only dowry they bring to their
husbands.'

Kerry stared at him. She bit her
bottom lip until it hurt. She wished she
hadn't mentioned it now. He would
hate her for knowing about Roberto.

'Well,' he insisted, 'what is it Leora
knows? It cannot be about us, because I
was hardly aware of it myself until
today, and I rather believe it was the

same for you. Please explain what you mean, and quickly.'

'She knows about Roberto,' Kerry answered in a small whisper.

'Roberto? Who is Roberto?'

He sounded genuinely perplexed. Kerry looked at him sharply. Perhaps Leora was right; likenesses could be passed down for centuries.

'He is known as Roberto Penaro.' He frowned and said nothing. 'You really don't know, do you, Carlos?'

He looked at her hopefully. 'Is he in love with Leora?'

At that Kerry threw back her head and laughed. Her laughter was tinged a little with hysteria. Carlos caught her by the shoulders and shook her fiercely.

'Kerry, stop it! Do you want everyone to come out here and find us together?'

She did stop laughing then. 'Yes,' she said ferociously.

'Perhaps if your fiancée finds us here together, with your precious code of ethics, she might not want to marry you any more.'

She looked into his anxious face and buried her head in his shoulder, and like a fool began to cry. He held her close in his arms, cradling her against him as if she were a baby.

'Oh, darling, I'm so sorry,' she sobbed, 'but I was so sure he was yours.'

She sat up again as he handed her a handkerchief. 'My what?'

'Your child,' she said patiently as she dried her eyes.

'My mind was always so full of you that I immediately thought he was yours. That's the only explanation I can think of.'

'Ah, so he is a child.' His face cleared.

'He lives with Senora Penaro and he looks very much like you. Leora visits them often and she seemed so, edgy when she saw me with him.'

'Many people around here have Ramiros blood in their veins. My great-great grandfather was a notorious rake. His favourite sport was the local girls. But, still, I should like to see this Roberto if there is such a striking likeness. You say he lives with Senora Penaro?'

'According to Leora she just looks after him, but Luis says Roberto is Senora Penaro's grandchild.'

'He certainly isn't mine.'

He kissed the hand he held tightly in his own and looked at her intently. Kerry felt the tears pricking in her eyes again. She put her arms round his neck, keeping close to him for a moment or two and then she drew away.

'I'm sorry I said what I did about you and Leora. I know it isn't mercenary of you to marry her. You'd marry her if she were poor if your father had arranged it.'

'I'm glad you understand. It isn't easy for me to let you go, Kerry. I just wish you hadn't come down here tonight. It would have been better if there had been nothing said between us.'

'We'll never know if that's true,' she sighed. 'I must leave here tomorrow, Carlos.'

He looked startled. 'So soon?'

'Is there any point in staying now? My relaxing holiday is over. All I can feel now is mounting frustration, and however long I do stay I must go home some time, the longer I leave it the harder it's going to be. You're very good at getting reservations at short notice. If you really love me you'll get me one for tomorrow.'

He kissed her again, hungrily, almost clumsily until she pulled away. 'Nothing's finished, darling,' she whispered, 'because it never really began.'

She stood up and before he could stop her she ran into the house and up the stairs. She was breathless and trembling when she reached her room. Throwing off her dressing gown she paused, fighting back the tears that were spilling onto her cheeks. She wasn't going to cry. There was nothing to cry about.

Desperate for something to do she rushed over to the window, to close the shutters, and froze on the spot when she saw Leora coming out of the house. She called for Carlos. Like her pet cat, thought Kerry spitefully. To her satisfaction there was no reply and she closed the shutters completely, standing for a moment with her back to them.

She was suddenly very tired. This morning seemed a long way away. A whole lifetime away.

Sleep did not come easily. She lay in the big Spanish bed, staring up at the ceiling, yet seeing nothing but the love, frustration and agony on his face. His kisses had fired her blood, awakening in her an entirely new awareness that would not let her sleep, and the birds were singing, regardless of her unrest, by the time slumber came to claim her.

11

It sounded as if someone had thrown a stone up at the shutters, hard enough to rouse her from sleep; or perhaps it was a bird passing too close to the window. She couldn't be sure.

She lay there for a few moments, reliving yet again the events of last night. Her emotions were still too new for her to be anything other than wonder-struck. When it was time to leave Valparaiso the hurt would start, but Kerry was determined not to think of that now. Enjoy the wonder of loving and being loved while you can, a little voice told her; the pain of losing it will last for ever.

Another stone hit the shutters. There was no doubt of it this time. She jumped out of bed and had to go halfway across the room to retrieve her dressing gown from where she had discarded it the night before. She pulled it round her quickly and went to open first the window and then the shutters. She pushed them back in one swift movement and went out onto the balcony. Her heart gave an uneven jerk as she looked down to find him standing beneath her balcony.

He was standing in the garden, his hands on his hips staring up at her.

'Have I slept very late?' she asked in amazement.

'It doesn't matter. Can you be down quickly?'

'Of course, but why?'

'I am going to see Senora Penaro.'

'You don't need me to be with you.'

'*Querida*,' he said wearily, 'I *want* you with me. Luis will be up at any time now and you know very well what that means. We may not have another chance to be together.'

Kerry bit her lip. She hardly needed the reminder. 'I'm not sure that I should. Last night was different, but we both know there's no . . . '

'We will be in the open all the time. It will look quite innocent.'

She laughed. 'I wasn't worried about that, but for your sake . . . '

'I'll risk it. Ten minutes — no longer — and I'll meet you at the stables. I'll have a horse made ready for you.'

He didn't wait for her to reply. She was still smiling when she went back into the bedroom.

It was a little more than fifteen minutes later when Kerry slipped, a little secretively, out of the house and through the garden. Despite her doubts about the sense of seeing Carlos alone, she couldn't help but feel excited at the prospect. Leaving him was a long way off; she didn't have to think about it just now.

He was waiting for her in front of the stables with his own chestnut mare and the horse she had ridden when she went to the village with Leora. He was longing as much as she, Kerry knew, to exchange a kiss, but for the sake of anyone who might be watching they had to be content just to clasp hands for a few moments. He helped her to mount before climbing easily into the saddle of his own horse.

He rides well, she thought, feeling the now familiar thrill she experienced whenever she looked at him. His soft leather riding boots were thrust into the stirrups, and wearing a pair of tight jeans and a white shirt that looked so well against the golden brown of his skin, he was nothing like the immaculately dressed man who seemed so cold and intimidating a few days ago; a lifetime ago . . .

It was not until they were riding slowly along the road to the village that she spoke at last.

'I can't help feeling that this visit to Senora Penaro's is just an excuse for us to go off together for an hour or so.'

'Naturally it is, but I am also curious to see this child.'

'It's amazing, isn't it, how a resemblance misses a generation or two and then occurs again?'

'It can be startling at times too. There is an old man in the village; when I see him, sometimes it's almost as if I am seeing my own father again, and yet he is no relation — not officially, that is.'

'Your great-great grandfather must have been quite a character.'

'He was known as the Casanova of the valley. Our family history is full of odd characters though. One day I will tell you . . . '

'Did you make any enquiries about a flight home for me?'

He didn't look at her. The workers they passed on the road paused to sweep off their straw hats as they rode past. Panniered donkeys drew into the side of the road so that they could ride unhindered.

'There is a reservation for you on this evening's flight to London.'

This evening. No time to brood.

'You're very efficient,' she said briskly.

'Shall I drive you to the airport?'

She was about to say, 'Yes, yes

236

please,' but instead she hesitated, their eyes met and hers filled with tears so she could hardly see him at all.

'No, Carlos, not you. Let Luis take me, or better still, a stranger so I don't have to keep up a cheerful appearance.'

He nodded wordlessly and as they entered the village she rode ahead along the narrow streets where dozens of children played and the women seemed to do all their chores out of doors. But everyone, the children included, fell into a respectful silence until they had passed.

When they reached Senora Penaro's house he dismounted and tethered his mare loosely to a post while Kerry waited to be lifted down. He held her tightly around the waist.

'I wish I could kiss you now,' he said as he set her down on the ground.

'You would cause quite a scandal if you did,' she said in a shaky voice, glancing round at the great number of women who were watching them.

She walked away from him, towards

Senora Penaro's house. Then she stopped and he caught up with her. 'Are you sure you want to go in?'

'Why not? Senora Penaro will be most honoured to see us.'

Senora Penaro did not look honoured; she looked surprised and more than a little flustered to see them, but quite a number of her neighbours were looking on with a considerable degree of envy at the honour Carlos had conferred upon her.

'*Buenas dias*, Don Carlos,' she gasped as she stood aside to let him inside. 'This is indeed an honour.'

Senora Penaro led them wordlessly into the house. The main room was, apart from the kitchen and a bedroom upstairs, the only room. The furniture was few and spartan, the walls white-washed to a startling degree of cleanliness, and the wooden table was scrubbed white.

She brought out a flacon of wine and poured the liquid into two glasses. Kerry followed Carlos's example and accepted the old lady's hospitality. Not to do so would have constituted an insult.

Carlos enquired as to the old lady's health and she answered politely, although Kerry sensed her unease in the way her eyes kept darting to the door. All eyes turned as Roberto himself came bursting into the room. His natural excitement faltered and died at the unexpected sight of visitors in his home.

Carlos watched the child with interest and Kerry could hardly suppress her amusement as his eyes widened in surprise, and then he looked at her.

'Olà, Roberto,' he said, transferring his attention back to the child who hung his head shyly.

The old woman scolded him with a quick torrent of words and he answered without looking up. 'Buenas dias, senor.'

Carlos's eyes narrowed suddenly. 'Venga, Roberto.'

The child hesitated but urged on by

Senora Penaro he went slowly up to Carlos who examined the medallion carefully. Then he looked up at Kerry.

'Have you seen this before?'

'It looks very much like the one Ferdy always wore. I gave that one to Dona Elvira when I arrived. But surely San Fernando medallions are quite common, aren't they?'

'This is Fernando's.' He smiled at Roberto, saying, 'Run along and play. Roberto.' He pressed a coin into his hand. 'Have an ice-cream and come back later.'

The child looked to Senora Penaro for permission. Stiffly she inclined her head and Roberto beamed excitedly before running out of the room. When he had gone Carlos glanced at Senora Penaro who was standing, eyes downcast, and then he looked at Kerry.

'Leora bought that medallion for his twenty-first birthday. I remember it quite clearly.'

Kerry's eyes grew wide. '*Leora* bought it?'

Kerry had never seen him look so grim since the day she had arrived, as he did when he fixed Senora Penaro with his steely stare.

'Who gave Roberto this medallion, Senora Penaro?'

'Dona Elvira,' the woman answered without looking up. 'She is fond of the boy.'

The door opened again and reluctantly Kerry drew her eyes away from the old woman's guilt-ridden face to see Leora standing in the doorway. Her face was a picture of dismay. She had turned so pale that her skin was the colour of her white blouse, a stark contrast to the deep black of her riding habit. Kerry, for one moment, thought she was going to faint but obviously Leora was made of sterner stuff, for she managed to smile faintly as she came further into the room.

'You two are a couple of early birds to be visiting Senora Penaro at this time of the morning. She is very honoured, Carlos. You will have to honour other families too after today.'

She fingered her riding whip nervously but otherwise seemed in perfect control of herself. Carlos, who had got to his feet when Leora appeared, remained standing.

'We were just wondering why Roberto had been given Fernando's medallion — the one you bought him. My mother is not usually so indiscriminately generous with family property.'

Leora grew pale again. She licked her lips in a nervous gesture and glanced at Senora Penaro who began to babble incoherently, waving her hands expressively in the air. Leora's face crumpled in distress and then she snapped 'Silencio,' and the woman fell silent.

Carlos looked from the old woman to Leora. 'Why do you silence her? I am beginning to be more intrigued by this business. Have you ever met the boy's parents, Leora?'

Leora sank down into a chair and waved her hand at the old woman. 'Leave us, please, senora. I wish to speak to Don Carlos myself.'

'Leora,' he prompted when the woman had gone from the room.

Suddenly and unexpectedly Leora turned away as sobs began to rack her body. She buried her head in her arms and sobbed heart-brokenly. Both Kerry and Carlos were completely astonished. Kerry glanced around her, unable to watch Leora's distress, and her eyes alighted on a scrap of paper which had been carelessly discarded on the floor.

Carlos put his arms around Leora's heaving shoulders. 'Leora, *carina*,' he said gently, 'what is it? Tell me. We have no secrets between us. What is it you are trying to hide? There is no shame in having a favourite in the village.'

Kerry stooped down and picked up the paper. It was a painting of a horse, a childish painting but a good one. Children were fascinated by many things; in more sophisticated places it was often cars; here horses were more common. And Roberto liked to portray them in everything. Kerry stared at the

243

picture and recalled Roberto's quick, clever fingers as he modelled the horse. She remembered too Ferdy talking of such things as the importance of balance and composition in a painting.

So sudden was the shock of realisation that her throat became dry and she could not speak. She stared at the painting until it became distorted before her eyes. The truth had been staring at her too, since the day she had first set eyes on Roberto, but it had been easier to believe something else.

Carlos was looking at Leora anxiously as the girl dabbed daintily at her eyes. She suddenly became aware of Kerry's unbelieving stare and she stared back, boldly, losing not a mite of that pride and arrogance so evident in her manner at all times. 'Why are you looking at me like that?'

'Because I know now why Ferdy left home.' She held up the painting. 'Roberto did this, Leora. He's very talented for a small boy, don't you think?'

Leora took the painting and seemed to stare at it for an age, although it could only have been a mere second or two. 'Of course,' she said in an even voice, 'Roberto is Fernando's son.' She looked at Kerry with eyes filled with hatred. 'You were determined to find out, weren't you? Well what good has it done you to let it be known now?'

She looked then at Carlos who seemed to be suffering from shock. At last he spoke and his voice was shaking with anger. 'This child is Fernando's son? Why wasn't I told?'

'There were reasons,' murmured Leora.

'Yet *you* knew.' Carlos laughed. 'I can't believe Fernando, of all people, and Rosa Penaro . . . '

Leora looked at him and laughed again. Her eyes flashed with some of her old spirit. 'Oh Carlos, how can you be so blind about your own brother? Rosa Penaro has been married quite respectably in Madrid for the past six years. I am Roberto's mother. Even now I have to spell it out for you.'

The arrogance crumbled again and Kerry hated to be witness to it. Leora began to cry softly again as Carlos stared at her, unable to speak. Kerry felt the tears pricking at her own eyes and she turned away to cover them with her hand.

'I am glad you know, Carlos,' Leora sobbed. 'I am so tired of pretending. All I want now is my child and no more pretending, no more sly and secret visits, being treated as a stranger by my own son.'

Kerry was forgotten in the corner. Carlos had recovered a little from his own shock and he went up to Leora and stroked her hair gently.

'Leora, tell me about it. Why didn't I know about it? How could I have *not* known?'

She brushed a few stray strands of hair from her tear-streaked face. It was the first time Kerry had seen her less than immaculate in appearance.

'Fernando and I were always in love,

ever since I could remember. We wanted to be married but Dona Elvira said we couldn't. I was betrothed to you and Fernando was to marry Sofia — our fathers had decreed it. We were too honourable to go against her decision but we were still in love and we did meet alone at almost every opportunity. Living in a house together made it very easy, and we were young and impatient.'

She stared unseeingly ahead, still holding Carlos's hands. 'It was all so marvellous and romantic, we never thought about the possible consequences. When I found out about . . . Roberto, I realised then what I had done was very wicked. My shame would be known throughout the valley and taint you all, Dona Elvira, you, Luis, Maria-Theresa and Maria Consuela. I had shamed the family that cared for me as its own and I was prepared to do anything I could to make amends for my wickedness.'

She looked up at him appealingly. He

released his hands and then went to sit down again. Kerry found herself staring at a collection of copper utensils which were hanging on the wall. They shone so brightly she could see her face in them, bloated and distorted and totally unreal.

'It took all my courage to face Dona Elvira,' Leora went on. 'I asked her what I must do and she told me nothing must change. I was to have the child and then come back and continue as before. This way no one would know of it, and we would be spared the shame. I could see that it was the only thing to do, so that is what I told Fernando.'

'He wouldn't accept it at first, but he no longer mattered. I was almost insane with remorse. If I married him everyone would know. It would kill Dona Elvira. I had to do as she asked.'

She put one hand to her head. 'That was when he went away.' Her voice was near to breaking point again. 'He said he would never come back, and I knew he meant it.'

'Dona Elvira took me away. I'd always suffered with migraine and it seemed a good time to look for a 'cure'. We never stayed long enough in one place to invite questions.'

'We came back to Spain but avoided the places we were known. Roberto was born in Madrid. Dona Elvira had already arranged for Senora Penaro to care for the child. I insisted on that; to be able to see him whenever I wished. That was the only way it would be bearable. When he was old enough to leave me Senora Penaro came and brought him back here.' Her face grew hard. 'And I came back too, to prepare to be the awe-inspiring mistress of Casa Ramiros!'

Carlos looked at Kerry at last and their eyes met and held for a moment before he stood up and went across to Leora.

'What do you want to do now, *carina*? Whatever you want is possible now. I will make sure of it. My mother did what she thought was right, but it was a great mistake.'

Leora smiled slightly and drew a deep sigh. It was as if a great load had been lifted from her shoulders.

'We cannot bring back the past. We can only make sure of the future. I shall take Roberto and Senora Penaro to my house at San Sebastian. You are of course relieved of any obligation to me.'

'No, Leora, that isn't true. That will never be true. What I feel for you is still the same and always will be. Roberto is my nephew. I still want to marry you.'

'I don't want to marry you, Carlos. I never gave up hoping that Fernando would come back to me, even though I never heard from him or even knew where he had gone until he wrote to say he was getting married. Even then I didn't give up hope.'

'I came here looking for something of Ferdy,' Kerry said at last. 'There was so much I didn't understand about him, but I never imagined it was this; that he really loved someone else — or perhaps I did.'

Leora looked at her. All that fierce hatred was gone. 'I blamed you for keeping him from me. I resented you being here, your right to be here as Fernando's fiancée. But it was all my fault. He wanted to marry me but I didn't have the courage to go against Dona Elvira, and I had to suffer the consequences. It is just.'

'I think you've been very brave,' answered Kerry, and looking at Carlos she added, 'I don't think I could have had such strength of will.'

'Not any more,' she murmured. 'In the future I'm going to do what is best for Roberto. That will be my only consideration.'

She raised her eyes and looked at Carlos. 'Please, I would like you to look after my financial affairs if you will.'

'Of course,' he assured her as he drew away. 'You have no need to ask.'

Roberto came running in at that

moment. From the appearance of his face it looked as if he had bought more than one ice-cream with the money Carlos had given him.

Kerry went across the room and outside into the bright sunshine without saying a word to either of them. She filled her lungs with air and let it out slowly. It was like waking up from a strange dream in which the people all behaved out of character.

Now the truth was out at last and they all could be themselves again. There were no more secrets, no more guilt — just happiness. It seemed that the sun was shining brighter than ever today.

Carlos came out of the house, closing the door softly. The door closed behind her and she turned to see him. He stood just outside the doorway, for the moment staring down at the ground thoughtfully.

'Is Leora all right now?' she asked hesitantly.

He looked up at her, smiled and

nodded. 'She has what she really wants, so she cannot help but be all right.'

'Your mother is really an amazing woman to go through all this with Leora for what she believed was right. In her own way she has suffered as much for it as Leora.'

He frowned and stared into the distance. 'This decision of Leora's will come as a shock to her, but she will recover, especially as matters are now as they should be.'

He looked at her then and put his hands on her shoulders. 'Duty is a fine thing but human nature must be taken into account sometimes. I realise that more than ever now. I love you, Kerry.'

'That's the first time you've said that.'

'It's the first time I have had the right. Will you stay?'

'You do realise that if Leora doesn't marry, Roberto will eventually have all her inheritance?'

'That is how it should be.'

She looked at him anxiously. 'All I

have to give is my heart.'

He reached out and took her hand in his. 'That, *carina*, is all I shall ever want.'

THE END

We do hope that you have enjoyed reading this large print book.

Did you know that all of our titles are available for purchase?

We publish a wide range of high quality large print books including:
Romances, Mysteries, Classics
General Fiction
Non Fiction and Westerns

Special interest titles available in large print are:
The Little Oxford Dictionary
Music Book, Song Book
Hymn Book, Service Book

Also available from us courtesy of Oxford University Press:
Young Readers' Dictionary
(large print edition)
Young Readers' Thesaurus
(large print edition)

For further information or a free brochure, please contact us at:
Ulverscroft Large Print Books Ltd.,
The Green, Bradgate Road, Anstey,
Leicester, LE7 7FU, England.
Tel: (00 44) **0116 236 4325**
Fax: (00 44) **0116 234 0205**

Other titles in the
Linford Romance Library:

A HEART DIVIDED

Sheila Holroyd

Life is hard for Anne and her father under Cromwell's harsh rule, which has reduced them from wealth to poverty. When tragedy strikes it looks as if there is no one she can turn to for help. With one friend fearing for his life and another apparently lost to her, a man she hates sees her as a way of fulfilling all his ambitions. Will she have to surrender to him or lose everything?

SAFE HARBOUR

Cara Cooper

When Adam Hawthorne with his sharp suit and devastating looks drives into the town of Seaport, Cassandra knows he's dangerous. Not only do his plans threaten to ruin her successful harbourside restaurant, but also Adam stirs painful memories she'd rather forget. When Cassandra's sister Ellie turns up, in trouble as usual, Cassandra needs all her considerable strength to cope. But will discovering dark secrets from Adam's past change Cassandra's future? And will he be her saviour or her downfall?

THE HAPPY HOSTAGE

Charles Stuart

When an agreement is made with the U.S.A. to build missile bases in Carmania, Elisabeth Renner and her friends plot to kidnap the American ambassador to Carmania and force the agreement to be cancelled. However, they get the wrong man: Charles Gresham, a budding British business tycoon. And he soon finds himself sympathising with his pretty captor. Then Elisabeth reluctantly decides to call it all off, and things really go wrong — when Charles doesn't want to be released!